"Is This So Bad?" He Asked Her.

She strove to answer him with the withering contempt she felt the occasion demanded, but she wanted badly to feel his mouth against hers again, parting her lips in an easy conquest that delighted even while it dismayed her. How could she give in to him like this? And, if she did, what else might he want from her?

He was a stranger! she reminded herself. She had to stop him before she lost her head entirely.

ELIZABETH HUNTER

uses the world as her backdrop. She paints with broad, colorful strokes; yet she is meticulous in her eye for detail. Well known for her delightful characters, she is internationally loved by her loyal and enthusiastic readers.

Dear Reader:

Silhouette has always tried to give you exactly what you want. When you asked for increased realism, deeper characterization and greater length, we brought you Silhouette Special Editions. When you asked for increased sensuality, we brought you Silhouette Desire. Now you ask for books with the length and depth of Special Editions, the sensuality of Desire, but with something else besides, something that no one else offers. Now we bring you SILHOUETTE INTIMATE MOMENTS, true romance novels, longer than the usual, with all the depth that length requires. More sensuous than the usual, with characters whose maturity matches that sensuality. Books with the ingredient no one else has tapped: excitement.

There is an electricity between two people in love that makes everything they do magic, larger than life—and this is what we bring you in SILHOUETTE INTIMATE MOMENTS. Look for them this May, wherever you buy books.

These books are for the woman who wants more than she has ever had before. These books are for you. As always, we look forward to your comments and suggestions. You can write to me at the address below:

Karen Solem
Editor-in-Chief
Silhouette Books
P.O. Box 769
New York, N.Y. 10019

ELIZABETH HUNTER
Fountains of Paradise

Silhouette **Romance**

Published by Silhouette Books New York

America's Publisher of Contemporary Romance

For Vi-jay,
and for my mother, who was there.

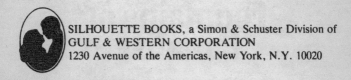

SILHOUETTE BOOKS, a Simon & Schuster Division of
GULF & WESTERN CORPORATION
1230 Avenue of the Americas, New York, N.Y. 10020

ISBN: 0-671-57218-0

First Silhouette Books printing, April, 1983

10 9 8 7 6 5 4 3 2 1

Map by Ray Lundgren

America's Publisher of Contemporary Romance

Printed in the U.S.A.

Other Silhouette Books by Elizabeth Hunter

The Lion's Shadow
Bride of the Sun
A Touch of Magic
Written in the Stars
One More Time
A Silver Nutmeg
London Pride

From Ceylon to Paradise, according to native tradition, is forty miles; the sound of the fountains of Paradise is heard there.

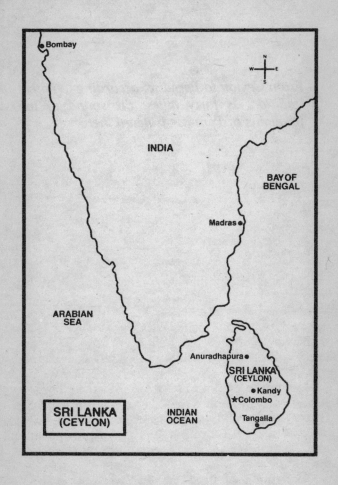

Chapter One

Exactly ten-thirty-five in the morning, and the great, wide-bodied aeroplane came slowly down out of the sky, topping the tall coconut trees by what seemed like only a few feet, and touched down on the island of Sri Lanka, the resplendent land, shaped like a teardrop of land shed from the subcontinent of India into the Indian Ocean.

Most of the passengers were going on to Singapore and only turned round to frown as Michal Brent joined the small group of people who had come to the end of their journey, blinking in the hot sunlight as the doors were opened to allow them to disembark.

She should have been bubbling over with excitement, but, instead, she felt slightly sick and her knees had developed a decided wobble, as if they were threatening not to carry her through Customs and out to the waiting Mr. van der Aa, whom she had never met and whom she was sure she wouldn't like, and even more sure that he wouldn't like her.

Well, who would, under the circumstances? *She* was not the girl he had been expecting to fly out to marry him. He hadn't been expecting her to come at all, or so Michal had convinced herself during the long flight from Europe. There had been no spare seat on the aeroplane, so it stood to reason that if Marika had come, there would have been no room for Michal—and no ticket, either, she suspected.

She had been a fool to believe Marika in the first place. Marika was as Dutch as Michal was English, but they had befriended one another at the boarding school to which they had both been sent: Marika to improve her English; Michal for the convenience of her family, because her parents had already been showing the signs of the breakdown in health that had resulted in their early deaths, leaving Michal to fend for herself as best she could.

And a very good "best" she had made of it. From an early age, she had been fascinated by design. She had gained for herself a thorough training—first in design, in general, and then in the design and setting of jewellery, in particular. It was because of this that she had been so tempted when Marika had pleaded with her to accompany her to Ceylon, or Sri Lanka as it was now called, where the Dutch girl was to become the wife of the man her family had determined she was to marry. At first Michal had been shocked by Marika's easy submission to her parents' wishes. She, herself, could never have brought herself to marry a man she had never met. Never, never! She had to admit, though, when Marika had pointed it out to her, that she had not been brought up in one of those small enclosed Dutch villages, either Protestant or Catholic, whose residents never mixed outside their own narrow societies, not even with the village next door. Apparently, the van der Aas had originally come from Marika's village, and their brides had been sent out to them from that same village ever since.

Of course, it might have occurred to Michal that Marika was a little too unconcerned at being sent halfway round the world to marry a man she had never met. Marika's family had never gone outside their village, but Marika had. Marika had been sent to school in England and was quite as unlikely as Michal was to submit to any such arrangement. If only Marika had said something to Michal of what she had meant to do! If only—

But Marika had said nothing. When Michal had got to the airport, there had been no sign of Marika, but Michal hadn't worried unduly, for Marika was always late for everything. It had only been when she had seated herself on board the aeroplane that Marika's letter had been delivered to her, and then the letter hadn't been for her; it had been addressed to Hendrik van der Aa, and scribbled on the back had been a message for Michal. *Thanks for going in my place,* it had read. *You might get some fun out of it! Good luck!*

Good luck, Michal thought now, was what she was going to need. A letter wasn't much protection when

11

it was all she had to divert the Dutchman's anger from her vulnerable head. She shouldn't have come! She should have turned right round and walked off the aeroplane there and then. She didn't know why she hadn't. Even less did she know how she was going to explain it all to Marika's Hendrik van der Aa.

How to explain to him how much this visit to Sri Lanka had meant to her? Famous for the quality of the gems to be found there, especially the sapphires, considered by many to be the finest in the world, Michal had seen it as a turning point in her career. Who, back home, was going to trust such gems to the care of a designer without experience? She would have had to spend years and years working under somebody else before her opportunity would have come. Now, with any luck, she would be able to buy the jewels herself and show what she could do without being beholden to anyone—except the unknown Hendrik van der Aa!

It was hot and humid outside. Michal was uncomfortable in the English winter clothes she was still wearing. With increasing nervousness, she walked across the short distance to the airport buildings and allowed herself to be bustled through the formalities necessary in all foreign ports. She had no foreign currency with her with which to pay for a porter, so she picked up her own suitcase and carried it out past the vigilant eyes of a policeman, through the swinging doors, and out into the colourful crowd outside.

For a moment, such was the tumult all about her, she couldn't hear what the man was trying to say to her. Then she realised she was staring at him and made a conscious effort to tear her eyes away from his face. What a formidable individual he looked!

"No, no, I'm not Miss Stove. I'm a friend of hers, Michal Brent. I'm terribly sorry!"

He changed from Dutch to English with an ease that made Michal swallow hard. She found herself looking at him again, as if his face had some irresistible attraction for her. He was incredibly fair—his hair would not have looked amiss on a young child, and his eyes were the bright green of jade. Only his skin bore witness to the land where he had chosen to live. It was the warm colour of toast, accentuating the whiteness of his teeth.

"What have you to be sorry for, Miss Brent?"

Michal spread her hands in a comprehensive gesture, having been relieved of her suitcase by a grinning porter.

"Everything. She hasn't come—and I shouldn't have come, either. I was coming with Marika to see her married, but she didn't come. I don't think she ever meant to come. Why should she, when she'd never met you? She gave me a letter for you."

Michal searched for the pale pink envelope that Marika favoured in her handbag, producing it with a flourish. "Here it is!" she said with a sigh of relief.

He read the note to her first, his eyes crinkling at the corners. "You have greater courage than she, perhaps?" he remarked. "You hadn't met me, either."

Michal stared at him in disbelief. "I'm English!"

"Yes, I'd noticed. You are Marika's English friend?"

Michal nodded in relief. She wished he wouldn't

13

look at her in quite that knowing, amused way, but she could hardly complain, for she had certainly looked at him. She had been so astonished by his fairness—and other things. It was impossible not to wonder what Marika would have made of such a man, but—and the unbidden thought made her blush—he was infinitely more a man than the boy her Dutch friend had been running round London with when she had last seen her.

"I see," Mr. van der Aa murmured. "It's your nationality which is to protect you from the consequences of launching yourself into my home in Marika's place." His teeth glinted in the strong sunlight. "You won't be the first Briton to have made that mistake."

Michal blinked, her heart hammering. She wondered if the muscles in his arms were as hard as they looked. She lowered her gaze to her clenched fists, which clutched her handbag.

"It's unkind of you to tease me," she forced herself to say. "I didn't know she wasn't coming—and you did say she could bring a friend with her to see her married. It isn't as if I came without an invitation. It wasn't my fault she didn't come!"

He walked in silence beside her towards a rather battered Vauxhall car, opening the door of the passenger's seat for her, then tipping the porter, who had stowed her luggage away in the boot at the back. Michal winced away from him as he got in beside her. She averted her eyes to the window, trying to think of something else besides the way his obvious masculinity was affecting her. It was a forlorn task. She was as conscious of the green jade

14

of his eyes when she was not looking at him as she was when she was looking into their depths. How odd, she thought, that such a man should seek marriage with a girl he had never met. He couldn't have been short of feminine admiration in any society!

"Tell me," he said, slipping the car easily into gear, "how long have you known that Marika was not coming with you?"

"Not until I was on the aeroplane."

His mouth tightened dangerously. "You should choose your friends more carefully."

"And you your wives!" Michal retorted.

He cast her a sidelong glance that was as comprehensive as it was masculine. "I'm not complaining about the exchange. You are better looking than the photos I have of Marika."

Michal was annoyed to feel herself blushing. She felt a mess after the long flight, her chestnut hair falling down her back, as it had long ago escaped its knot at the back of her neck. Nor did she have any makeup on. Her long, thick lashes were black enough without any aids, but she doubted a pair of wide brown eyes made up for a shiny nose and a complete lack of lipstick on her trembling lips.

"You'd better read me Marika's letter. Is it in English or Dutch?"

"I don't know."

"Then find out," he commanded her.

The letter, she remembered, was in his pocket. She hesitated, annoyed by his slight smile as he realised her dilemma. He pulled out the crumpled envelope and handed it to her.

"It's in English," she admitted as she opened it.

15

"But I don't want to read it. It's a private matter between the two of you. It has nothing to do with me."

"Think not?" He took the letter from her and glanced down at it, slowing the car almost to a halt. "It has everything to do with you," he said finally. "You could call it a letter of introduction."

"Let me see!" Michal snatched at the thin piece of paper, tearing a corner as she did so. A brief scanning of the words was enough to convince her he was telling the truth, and that Marika had been unsparing in her praise of her friend. She was adaptable, healthy, and with a love of adventure, more suitable in every way for a life in a neglected paradise, far away from the civilised necessities of life that Marika required to be a feature of her own married life.

"How could she?" Michal moaned. She felt hot and cold all over and was horrified to discover she felt queazy on top of everything else. "I think you'd better stop the car!" she warned him.

He took one look at her face and did so. He leaned across her and opened her door, pushing her out of the car with firm hands, coming languidly round the car himself to join her at the side of the road.

"Feeling better?"

She nodded yes, then just as quickly shook her head negatively. "I feel terrible. How could she do this to me?"

He smiled with a lack of feeling she could only deplore. "Come home with me, and let what happens happen. Haven't you heard that here you're only forty miles from Paradise?''

"Paradise only means a garden, really, doesn't it?" she said inconsequentially.

"A Persian garden," he corrected her.

"I can't live in Paradise at your expense!" Michal exclaimed. "I came here to work!"

"Nevertheless, you're welcome to stay for a few days in my house without any strings attached. Are you ready to go on?"

She nodded, a smile beginning to tug at the corners of her mouth. "I don't suppose you want any strings, either?"

His green eyes hardened. "Don't be too sure of that. I have need of a wife, and you will do as well as Marika for that—better, if she is to be believed!"

Michal flounced back into the car. "I'm not about to be any man's wife!" She told herself he was teasing her and that she was a fool to take his alarming statement seriously, but she couldn't be quite sure, and her heart pounded painfully in her breast. She had never met anyone remotely like him before, never seen any man who could change the whole chemistry of her being at a mere glance from those jade-green eyes.

She was relieved when he made no attempt to engage her in conversation the whole way to Colombo. He allowed her to absorb her surroundings in peace, concentrating on his driving, which required a great deal of care, for the roads, whilst good, were narrow and full of cars, pedestrians, and animals. Indeed, there was little opportunity for them not to use the middle of the road, for the edges were crowded with coconut palms, villages, and encroaching undergrowth, making it necessary to hoot a warning every few seconds to make any progress at all. Michal was amused to notice that whilst the dogs and even the cows would move obligingly out of the way, the human beings would swerve from their elected path a few inches at most as the car rushed past them.

"I'm glad you like Sri Lanka," Hendrik said suddenly as they maneuvered their way through the streets of the capital.

"I haven't said I do," she pointed out.

"You have a very expressive face, Miss Brent."

She was put out that he should have taken the time to observe her reactions so closely. She felt more vulnerable than ever, and she was too tired at that moment to work out what she was going to do next.

"It's a bit different from the neatness of Holland," Hendrik said.

Michal looked out the window and thought it was very different from England, also. The slim-hipped men in their sarongs, a tube of cloth they folded into their waists, and the women in their own form of the same dress, would have looked out of place, indeed, in the wintry streets she had left behind in Europe.

"The Netherlands," Michal corrected him. "Marika doesn't like to hear her country called Holland. It's like referring to Scotland as England. You ought to know better!"

He cast her a mocking glance. "I'm too many generations removed from Europe to know these things. Here, they call us burghers. How will you like to be a burgher's wife?"

She knew now that he was teasing her. She even managed a laugh. "You haven't got the presence to be my idea of a burgher. Nor the wealth!"

He raised his eyebrows. "Marika gave you details of my bank balance, too?"

Michal flushed guiltily. "Of course not. I was judging by your car—and things like that. Besides, you're too young to have made much money yet." She took a deep breath, aware that she was making bad worse. "Burgher sounds so very middle-aged and respectable."

He looked amused. "Nevertheless, I'm a reasonably solid citizen. Very respectable, I assure you."

That wasn't her impression of him! He was far too dangerously attractive to be respectable, and solid was the last epithet she would have applied to him, unless it were to his muscles. They were solid enough and rippled expressively beneath his shirt, which stuck to his shoulders and back in the damp heat.

"So respectable you have to have a Dutch wife," she accused him, eager to have her revenge for the disturbing effect he had on her.

"It seemed a practical arrangement. If I had found someone to marry here, it would have been more romantic. But there was no-one. So why upset old customs that have always worked well in the past? As long as the girl wasn't committed to anyone else, I reckoned it might work very well. It did with my parents. Would it be so difficult for a woman to fall in love with me?"

Michal licked her lips nervously. "No," she said finally.

"Then why complain about a long-standing arrangement you know nothing about?"

Michal gasped with indignation. "It's so cold-blooded! It wouldn't do for me!"

"You're probably hungry," Hendrik returned calmly. "Everything seems impossible on an empty stomach."

"Even on a full stomach I couldn't marry a man I didn't love!" Michal insisted.

His teeth shone white in the sunlight. "No one has asked you to, Michal Brent. How come you have a boy's name? Was it your parents' idea of a joke?"

"It isn't a boy's name," she denied. "It's in the Bible. Michal was one of David's wives."

"Ah, yes," he remembered. "She objected to him dancing naked before the Ark of the Lord."

"Perhaps she had a point," Michal remarked dryly.

The jade eyes were greener than ever. "No! He should have persuaded her to join him. Would you dance with me?"

"And what would the elders of your church, choosing your wife for you back in Holland, say to that?" Michal demanded sharply.

Hendrik van der Aa laughed, shrugging his shoulders. "They wouldn't know. There'd be only you, and me, and the black, velvet night to see us."

Michal raised her chin. "My reactions would be exactly the same as the first Michal's!" she claimed. "I'd disapprove."

Green eyes held hers prisoner for a long moment.

"I wonder," he said. He touched her cheek with one finger and smiled. "You're too pretty to be as puritanical as the folks back home," he said.

Michal had always been convinced that there was a logical explanation for everything if one was prepared to search for it, so there had to be one for the extraordinary feelings that Hendrik van der Aa could let loose inside her just by giving a look from those strange green eyes. It didn't take her long to come up with an explanation. She was tired, she decided, bone-weary, and her mind and body were both confused by a combination of lack of sleep and jet lag. After a long sleep, a shower, and a change of clothes, he would become a perfectly ordinary man again, and less of a threat to her comfort and her future. It was absurd to suppose he was really a threat to her independence. How could he be? Marika might have put the idea into his head that Michal would do as well as a wife for him, but to suppose that either of them was seriously considering herself in such a role was just as laughable.

So, why did she jump every time he looked at her? And why did she tingle all over at the thought of those hands on the steering wheel caressing her?

She refused to think about him anymore. She turned her back on him and watched the passing scenery, instead. Cows lay in the middle of the road, chewing their cud, with humps on their backs and superior expressions on their faces. They were as sure of themselves as the calm-eyed dogs that went about their own business without any apparent reference to their owners. Most distinctive of all were the coconut palms, their curving trunks making beautiful patterns against the sea and the vast expanses of silver sand that edged it.

For a moment Michal forgot her caution. "I've never seen orange coconuts before," she said.

"They're the king coconuts. They're the best there are. During the war they were even used successfully instead of blood transfusions. There's not a part of the plant which isn't used. We value them very highly."

"Copra is a major export, isn't it?" Michal asked.

"Right, and coir ropes. There's a whole cottage industry engaged in soaking, washing, pounding, and turning the coir into string. You'll see lots of rope-walks by the side of the road before long."

There was one in the next village they came to, and Michal expressed her satisfaction at seeing such a thing for herself.

Hendrik's smile mocked her. "That's better," he commended her. "You have a mouth better made for kissing than sulking."

His words caused a shock wave to pass through her. "I'm very particular about whom I kiss," she informed him lightly.

"Do you think I could talk you into kissing me?"

"Certainly not!" she said.

His smile grew wider. "If I chose—"

"I do my own choosing!" she asserted.

His disbelieving silence rattled her badly. She could think of nothing but the green of his eyes and the smooth, attractive tan of his skin. What would it be like to be kissed by him?

"You don't look old enough to make such choices

on your own," Hendrik said after a pause. "And with that milkmaid's complexion, glossy hair as bright as a chestnut, and that wide-eyed, passionate look in your eyes, you are an invitation to trouble. I only wonder that your parents allowed you to travel so far by yourself."

"They're dead," she said baldly.

"I'm sorry." To her surprise, he sounded as though he meant it.

"They had me very late in life," she confided. "My mother was already ailing, and she died soon after I was born. My father died a couple of years ago. He was much older than my mother, and she was more than forty when I came along. My father thought it very unfair that she should have died first. He loved her very much."

"Was she beautiful, too?"

"She had hair like mine," Michal admitted.

He made no comment on that. Instead, he pointed ahead of them down the road. "Home is just round the corner. Has it seemed a long drive?"

On the contrary, it had gone by in a flash, bathed in an excitement she had never known before. She stretched her body lethargically and smiled to herself. Despite everything, she could only be glad she had come to Sri Lanka.

The house was on a finger of land that pointed out from the coastline, separating the sea from the mouth of the broad river that had meandered its way from the centre of the island, through all kinds of scenery to the mangrove swamps for the last few miles, broken only by the villages that used its waters as their highway to and from the coastal towns.

The house itself wasn't at all as she had imagined it to be. It was large, single-storeyed, and very grand, with Dutch gables above every window and a car-porch outside the front door that was as wide as most people's living rooms. Even better than the house was the garden, dipping away down a steep incline, a mass of flowering trees and ornamental bushes, full of private corners that might be Japanese, English, or as formal as some of the Continental gardens of Europe.

"It's beautiful!" Michal exclaimed, delighted. "What are those trees?"

"Temple flowers. Frangipani."

She was out of the car, breathing in deeply the fragrance of another bush. "And this?"

"Jasmine."

She touched the tiny, star-shaped flowers. "You have a gorgeous home, Mr. van der Aa. Perhaps the native tradition is true. I believe one might be able to hear the fountains of Paradise from here, after all."

He didn't answer her immediately. Then he finally said, "You'd better come inside and meet Belle. She was expecting Marika. She'd even learned a Dutch phrase of greeting for her. But she won't mind if you answer her in English."

Michal's lips trembled with an uncontrollable nervousness. "Mr. van der Aa, I'm sorry Marika didn't come, but don't be too disappointed. I know you'd gone to a lot of trouble to make her welcome, but she wouldn't have appreciated it. She never notices gardens—she doesn't even much like flowers, not even tulips! She'd have been like a fish out of water here. She only likes cities and coffee bars and walking round the shops with her friends."

"You'd better call me Hendrik," he said.

Michal bit her still-trembling lip. "You're much better off without her!" she blurted out.

He shrugged his shoulders. "Perhaps I am, perhaps not. I am willing to be persuaded either way. Come inside, *meisje,* and welcome. We will have time to talk about Marika's defection after you've caught up on your sleep."

Chapter Two

Michal came slowly out of a deep sleep, wondering why she felt such a zest for life. The answer came to her in a flash. She wanted to see more of Hendrik van der Aa. She lay on her back and thought about him in what she hoped was an objective manner. That he had an unfortunate effect on her was obvious, for she wouldn't be in Sri Lanka long enough for any relationship to develop between them. And that brought her to the next problem. How was she to get back to England when she had very little money and even less time to work her passage home, as she had originally planned?

She became aware of a small figure about the room, trying to discover if she was awake.

"Yes?" Michal asked lazily.

"Excuse me, madam," the shadow whispered. "Shall I bring you tea?"

Michal recognised Hendrik's housekeeper's diminutive figure and smiled at her. "Is it tea time?" she marvelled. "I must have slept for hours! But you mustn't wait on me, Belle. You have enough to do without that!"

Belle put dimpled fingers up to her mouth. "It's late, very late. Mr. Hendrik ate his dinner long ago, but you were still sleeping. Will you eat something now?"

"No, thank you," Michal said. "But I should like some tea. Shall I come to the kitchen?"

"If you will," Belle agreed with satisfaction. "It's almost my son's bedtime, but you have time to meet him if you come at once."

Michal was surprised. Belle looked far too young to have any children of her own. "How old is he? And what's his name?" she asked.

"His name is Saman. He's nine years old. His father has been dead for eight years. Since then I am working for Mr. Hendrik, and Saman lives here with me."

Michal chuckled. "You must be older than you look!"

Belle giggled. "Older than you! I am nearly thirty years old already." She gave Michal a languishing look out of the corners of her dark eyes. "You like Mr. Hendrik?"

"Don't you?" Michal countered.

A stifled giggle greeted this sally. "You are very funny, madam. Of course, we all like Mr. Hendrik!

27

He's a beautiful man—rich and generous, and always kind. To be his wife will be a good thing for madam."

Michal jerked her head. "I'm not going to marry him!"

Belle's face went blank. "You are here," she pointed out. "Miss Marika didn't come. I myself asked Mr. Hendrik if he was pleased with you. He laughed and said he hadn't made up his mind yet whether to keep you or throw you back." Belle shrugged her shoulders. "Why should he send you home when he needs a wife, and you're here?"

Michal sat on the edge of her bed and tried to gather her scattered wits into some kind of order. "One doesn't choose a wife as one chooses a fish," she pointed out carefully. "Nor a husband, either!" she added with spirit.

Belle was unimpressed. "Why else did you come so far?" She smiled sweetly down at the startled English girl. "Excuse me, madam, but I think the kettle will be boiling. Can you find the kitchen by yourself?"

Michal was still sitting where Belle had left her five minutes later. The time had come to assert herself—that was for sure. Why, then, did she feel as though she had already lost the battle. She *knew* Hendrik van der Aa had no intention of keeping her in Ceylon a moment longer than necessary. He was probably expecting her to buy her ticket home as soon as she had recovered from the journey out. There was only one trouble with that—she simply didn't have the money to do so. It had cost her most of her savings just to live when she had given up her job in order to accompany Marika out to her bridegroom. Marika had assured her she would be welcome to stay round as long as it took to get together a collection of her own designs in jewellery to take back to England with her. Optimistically, Michal had thought she could work hard enough to do that and to earn enough for her fare home. She had thought she had all the time in the world, and now that time was reduced to a matter of a few hours.

She flung a dressing gown over her revealing nightgown and went to find the kitchen. Once Hendrik had got over the shock of her arrival without Marika, he might be prepared to help her. Judging by the size and quality of his home, he had the means.

Although Michal's thoughts were full of him, she was completely unprepared when he appeared at the other end of the corridor. She wrapped her dressing gown more closely about her slight figure, pausing to give him time to go away again, but he had seen her and was obviously waiting for her to come up level with him.

"Had a good sleep?"

She nodded. "Mr. van der Aa, when is the next flight back to England?"

He looked her up and down with a disagreeable thoroughness. "What's the hurry?"

"I can't stay here—not without Marika." She wished she could read his expression, but she couldn't. She felt more uncomfortable than ever. "Perhaps we could talk about it in the morning?" she suggested.

"What's there to talk about? You're here; Marika isn't. Isn't that the way you planned it?"

"No. I thought she was coming. I really did!"

He opened a door just beside him and gestured for her to precede him inside. It was difficult to avoid touching him as she went past him, and her colour was correspondingly high as she looked round the agreeable book-lined room, which was obviously where he did most of his work.

"Don't you think you might give Sri Lanka a try?" Hendrik's voice came to her from the doorway.

She turned to face him. "I haven't the money," she said baldly.

"That's what I thought." His tone was dry and a little contemptuous.

Suppose he really did believe that she had planned to take Marika's place?

"You weren't the only person Marika let down!" Michal retorted sharply. "She's put me in an impossible position—and you're making it worse!"

His green eyes flashed. "What am I doing? As a matter of fact, I'm beginning to think Marika may have done me a good turn. You look a dainty dish, indeed, in your night things."

She eyed him warily. "Don't be ridiculous!"

A smiled played at the corners of his lips. "What's ridiculous about the attraction between a man and a woman? It seems to me more like a stroke of luck for both of us."

"I'm going back to England."

"Are you?"

She nodded her head. "I have to go back to

England. I can't stay here without Marika. I only came to keep her company—"

"And to make your fortune."

"Well, yes," Michal admitted. "But that isn't possible now, is it?"

"I can think of a way," he began.

Her eyes flashed. "I'm sure you can! Well, you can just think again, Mr. van der Aa! Moreover, if you had an ounce of charity in your makeup, you'd advance me my fare back to Europe on the understanding that I repay you in monthly installments, which I would. Aren't Buddhists supposed to be renowned for their compassion?"

"I'm a Christian," Hendrik said.

She was glad of the change of subject. "I thought everyone here's a Buddhist. We saw several Buddhist temples along the way."

"Buddhists, Hindus, Christians—we all live in peace with one another in Sri Lanka."

"Then, of your *Christian* charity, won't you lend me the money to go home?"

His eyes narrowed. "No."

"Just like that?" she demanded.

"Just like that!"

Michal clenched her fists in exasperation. "What are you going to do with me?" she demanded.

"I haven't decided yet. A lot depends on you."

She was bitterly aware of her state of undress, which added to her vulnerability. Tears rushed towards the front of her eyes, and she blinked rapidly, anxious that he shouldn't see them. She was going to need all the pride in herself she could muster.

"You'll regret keeping me here!" she told him, lifting her chin.

"Maybe, but I don't think so."

"Why not?"

He took a step towards her, putting his hands on her shoulders and drawing her tight up against the broad expanse of his chest. The contact knocked the breath out of her body, giving her a sharp pain in her middle. She tried to shrug off his touch, but she could not. His hands slipped behind her back and held her even more closely against him.

"This is why not," he said against her ear.

His breath was warm, and the trail of his fingers against her neck and cheeks burnt with an anticipation she had never felt for any man before. Her lips trembled as she averted her face from his interested gaze, but not before she had caught a glimpse of the strong column of his throat, rising between broad shoulders. He had no right to be so . . . so masculine and attractive.

Her heart pounded in her breast as his mouth touched hers. His hands slipped beneath her gown, smoothing her cotton nightdress flat against her flesh.

"Is this so bad?" he asked her.

She strove to answer him with the withering contempt she felt the occasion demanded, but she wanted badly to feel his mouth against hers again, parting her lips in an easy conquest that delighted, even while it dismayed her. How could she give in to him like this? And, if she did, what else might he not want from her?

The taste and smell of him pervaded her whole being. His kiss became more demanding, depriving her of any thought, except her sudden and unexpected need for him. He was a stranger! she reminded herself desperately. She knew nothing about him—nothing at all. She had to stop him from ever kissing her again before she lost her head entirely.

But it was not she who ended the kiss, after all. He put her away from him, smiling deep into her tawny eyes.

"I think we'll deal with each other very well when you've come round to the idea, but you're not ready for more just now. Go and get your tea."

She tore herself out of his arms and stumbled towards the door. "I hate you!" she yelled at him over her shoulder. "I'll never be ready to so much as exchange the time of day with you!"

He stood with his hands on his hips, laughing at her. The hot colour went rushing to her face as her fury with him and with herself mounted to a new, unbearable height.

"I *hate* you!" she repeated.

"You're welcome," he replied politely, accompanying the words with a formal, Continental bow that would have been ridiculous in anyone less confident, less arrogant than Hendrik van der Aa. "Good night, Michal. Sleep well!"

She slammed the door behind her, annoyed to find that she was still shaking from the encounter. She would have her tea and, afterwards, she would stay the night, because she didn't know what else to do. When the morning came, she would be ready for the impossible Dutchman. She would show him once and for all that he had made a mistake in tangling with Miss Michal Brent.

To her shame, Michal slept the whole night through. The strange sounds of the tropical night did not interfere with her slumbers. Indeed, when she awoke, it was some time before she remembered the impasse that faced her that day.

A few muffled noises from the kitchen told her that Belle was already up, and perhaps so was the son she had been too late to meet the evening before. Michal dressed quickly and then entered the kitchen, asking what she could do to help.

Belle greeted her with a friendly smile. "Good morning, madam. You slept well, no?"

"Too well. I awoke ravenously hungry. Is there anything I can do?"

Belle's eyes filled with laughter. "Mr. Hendrik is on the terrace. I'll bring your breakfast there as soon as it's ready."

Michal was wondering how she could explain that she would rather not meet Hendrik quite yet, when a small boy came into the kitchen and, putting his palms together in front of him, bowed solemnly to them both.

"My son!" Belle introduced him proudly.

Michal murmured a "hello" to the boy, trying to keep the surprise she felt out of her voice, for he could hardly have been more different in looks from his mother. He was almost as fair as Hendrik, with a decided gold tinge to his hair and the tips of his eyelashes. Only his eyes came from his mother; they were as dark and as liquid as hers.

"His father is dead?" Michal asked on a note of doubt. Immediately, she wished she hadn't when she saw the look of intense misery cross Belle's expressive face.

"Yes, dead. My son has only me to guide him—and Mr. Hendrik. But my son doesn't wish to be a burgher. It's in his mind to enter the monastery."

"He's young enough to change his mind," Michal comforted her.

"He can go when he's ten years old. He'll get a good education in the monastery."

Michal was shocked that anyone so young should be allowed to make such a choice, yet it had once been the same in Europe before the freedom of childhood had been invented, releasing the young from being looked upon as tiny adults, with the same responsibilities and burdens as their elders.

Saman seemed to know exactly what Michal was thinking. A precocious smile curved his lips. "Welcome to Sri Lanka, Miss Brent," he said in a high, boyish treble. "You mustn't criticize my mother, because I know my own mind. I am older than both of you if you count my previous lives." He smiled sweetly at her. "Excuse me, but I must leave for school. I came for my mother's blessing."

Mother and son bowed to each other, intent only on themselves and the bond between them. Belle said something to him in Sinhala, then went on in English: "Have a good day, my son."

Saman bowed once more, including Michal in the gesture of respect, and then was gone with a flash of bare feet and a piercing whistle to catch the attention of his friends.

"You like my son?" Belle asked Michal, tears trembling on her lashes.

"You're lucky to have him," Michal responded warmly. "He's charming!"

Belle managed a smile. "In looks he favours his father, but his ways are his own. He will do well in the monastery."

"Does he have to stay forever?" Michal asked, secretly appalled.

"No, no. He can put off the robe any time he wishes, but Saman will want to stay. Every morning he asks for my blessing, and every morning I feel it is I who should be asking for his." She sighed again. "Go and join Mr. Hendrik, madam, and I'll bring your breakfast with his. Afterwards, if you're willing, his aunt would like to meet you."

"He has relatives living with him here?" Michal was startled into exclaming. "Oh, I'd much rather have my breakfast with her!"

"She's bedridden," Belle warned her, "but she'll be glad to have someone to pass the time with." Belle's eyes became suddenly blank. "Tante Willy came from the same village as Marika. She was looking forward to Marika's arrival, to talk about her many friends and relatives there. You won't be her first choice for a bride for Mr. Hendrik. She wanted him to marry one of her own."

"Can I have breakfast with her? I shan't upset her, because I have no intention of marrying her nephew!"

Belle threw her a piercing glance. "Mr. Hendrik

left instructions that you are to breakfast with him. D'you want papaw or pineapple? And how many eggs?"

Michal had never tried papaw, or pawpaw, or papaya, as it was sometimes called. She eyed the orange flesh cut from a fruit similar in looks to a melon and elected to have that. Belle put a large portion onto a plate, brushing off the black seeds from the centre, together with a slice of lime. "Take this with you, madam, and I'll bring your eggs in a minute."

Michal should have been quite ready to face Hendrik after her long, refreshing sleep, but the already familiar prickle of excitement rose within her at the sight of him. She had no more idea of how to handle him now than she had the evening before. He rose to his feet as she joined him on the verandah. She was uncomfortably aware of his powerful build. She didn't even have to look at him to know exactly how his hair grew out of his scalp, curling round the collar of his shirt in slightly damp tufts after his morning shower.

The intensity with which she felt his physical presence brought a belligerent slant to her mouth, denying it its usual smile.

"Good morning," she said abruptly.

Hendrik sat down again, raising an eyebrow at her. "Sleep well?"

She put her plate down on the table with a clatter. "Have you decided to send me home?"

"If you begin to show signs of distress at being kept here against your will. I've seen small signs of that as yet."

"I'm naturally brave," she said.

"Or eager for new experiences?"

Her eyes widened dramatically. "You flatter yourself. I'd like to explore Sri Lanka, but not our relationship. That's one experience I can do without."

A flash of green revealed his amusement and sent the colour racing up her cheeks. "You should have told me that yesterday evening," he observed dryly. "There wasn't much reluctance about you then."

Michal preferred not to answer that. As a jibe it was beneath contempt, certainly not something to argue about—especially as, so far, she had lost every verbal battle to this infuriating man.

An outrigger canoe, so narrow that its owner had to sit astride it, came slowly into view on the sea at the end of the sloping garden. The fisherman waved a friendly hand, the broad brim of his ancient hat flapping in the breeze.

"Do they catch much fish?" Michal asked.

Hendrik van der Aa nodded. "The fishing is excellent, but the fishermen are considered rather low caste, as they take life. Buddhism has no caste system of its own, but it made its appearance here with the South Indian invaders early on in Ceylon's history. It's not as rigid as it is in India, but it exists."

"I'd forgotten Buddhists don't approve of killing anything," Michal said. "They're right. I think it's wrong, too, but I haven't the courage of my convictions."

"I don't think a true Buddhist would go along with it being wrong," he told her. "They believe in cause and effect, not that an action is sinful in itself. After all, if there is no righteous God, wrong actions can't offend Him, but you can't escape the effects of what you, and what others do."

"Isn't Buddha a kind of god?"

"No. There've been several Buddhas, but they were all men. They were in no way redeemers. Every Buddhist has to work out his own salvation by his own efforts, through many lives, until he no longer hungers after life at all. It isn't really a religion at all, but a philosophy, a way of life."

"But the people worship Buddha," Michal objected. "I saw their temples as we drove along yesterday. Many of them had Hindu gods attached to them."

"Yes, they did. Buddhists respect Buddha, but they don't adore him. He was only a man, like the rest of us. Ordinary people hunger after gods, however. In many Buddhist shrines, the Hindu gods have succeeded in finding a niche for themselves. In most pictures of Buddha preaching, you can see the gods hanging out of heaven behind him to catch his words. Nobody minds. If you're a child in your needs in this life, why shouldn't you have toys to play with? In another life you'll understand the foolishness of those desires and be a little closer to the liberation all Buddhists ultimately seek."

Michal glanced at him from beneath her lashes. "Like Saman?" she suggested.

"You've met my young cousin?"

His cousin? Who, then, was Belle? "I know you have an aunt living here," Michal answered, bewildered.

"We're all related. Belle is my aunt's only son's widow. Saman is his son."

"Oh!" said Michal.

His expression hardened. "I suppose you leapt to another, less worthy conclusion?"

"I tried not to," Michal defended herself. "Belle said her husband was dead, and, of course, I believed her. But I didn't realise she was your cousin-in-law. Why does she call you Mr. Hendrik?"

"For the same reason she calls you madam. The Sinhalese have the best manners of any people I know."

Michal chewed on her lower lip. "I'm going to meet your aunt after breakfast. Are there any more shocks in store for me?"

He eyed her thoughtfully. "None I can think of. I must go. Finish your breakfast. I'll see you at lunchtime. It'll be interesting to find out what you make of us all. You may even want to become one of us!"

She stirred uncomfortably beneath that relentless green gaze. "I'll still want to go back to England," she maintained stoutly.

He tapped her lightly on the head, raising her chin with a finger until she was forced to meet his wry smile. "We'll see," he said.

"We won't see at all! You can't force me to stay

here!" She pushed his hand away with vigour. "I shall talk to your aunt about my going back to England. She will understand exactly why I can't stay here."

His lips curled into a smile. "She may. Tante Willy has a mind of her own."

Chapter Three

The view from Michal's room included a lengthy stretch of the river beyond. On the other side of the house, one could hear the sea pounding against the white sand of the beach, a deserted beach fringed with coconuts and piles of coral from the reef that was brought ashore and burned in kilns for making cement and other building products. It had a funny smell that Michal was not yet used to, but the river smelt as sweet as anyone could desire. Belle had told Michal she would sometimes be able to spot an iguana on its banks, or one of the crocodiles, but secretly she rather hoped she would never have to come face to face with the latter.

As she watched, she became aware of three birds perching on a dead piece of wood near the water. To see three kingfishers, as she presumed they were, was an unexpected cause for excitement. To see one would have made her day complete at home in England. A flash of blue marked the flight of one of the birds as it flew low over the water and returned to its perch. The next on, however, was not blue at all, but a brilliant jade-green that sparkled in the bright sunlight. Somewhere, recently, she had seen exactly that colour—why should this make her catch her breath? She leaned forward to get a better look.

"Tante Willy is waiting for you, madam." Belle's voice came from the doorway. "Shall I take you to her now?"

"Your mother-in-law?" Michal took a last look at the kingfishers and was rewarded by another flash of blue. "Yes, please. And please call me Michal; everyone does."

"Miss Michal," Belle compromised, wrinkling up her nose in disapproval.

Michal smiled at her. "You should have told me your husband was Hendrik's cousin, Miss Belle!"

"Oh, very well, Michal," Belle gave in. "What are you looking at?"

"Some kingfishers on the bank. I've never seen so many all at one time."

Belle looked where Michal was pointing. "One, no two, of those are bee-eaters, but there are many, many kingfishers living on the bank—herons, too, and painted stalks, and lots of sea birds." She paused. Then she went on: "It's of no interest now who my husband was. It was always arranged that he and Mr. Hendrik would share everything, and, after them, it would all go to Saman as their joint heir. Now it's clear he will need nothing more than the two robes of a *biku*, his begging bowl, and a pair of shoes. As my husband is dead, other arrangements have to be made."

"Which is why Hendrik decided to get married?"

"It's the custom in his family for them to send home to Holland for their wives." A fleeting glimpse of humour spread across Belle's face. "First Hans breaks that custom, and now, it seems, Mr. Hendrik will, too. Poor Tante Willy! Her village in Holland means so much to her, even though she hasn't seen it for years."

Michal was curious to meet Hendrik's aunt. She felt sorry for anyone compelled to spend all her days in bed, and was prepared to make allowances for any eccentricities Tante Willy might have cultivated by way of compensation. Nothing, however, had prepared her for the youthful looks of Wilhemina van der Aa, nor for the strong likeness the elder woman held to Marika. If she had been a few years younger, they could well have been sisters.

"*Goede Morgen,*" the woman on the bed greeted her.

Michal tried to answer, but no sound came out of her mouth. Tante Willy sighed lustily. "You don't speak Dutch? Anyone could make a stab at understanding 'good morning' and making some kind of an answer. Good heavens, girl, haven't you ever seen anyone in bed before?"

"Forgive me," Michal said in a rush, "but you even sound like Marika! You could almost be her twin!"

44

Tante Willy fixed Michal with a stare. "That must be your guilty conscience talking," she said flatly.

"I haven't got a guilty conscience," Michal denied stiffly. "It wasn't my fault that Marika backed out at the last moment. She preferred to stay with her boyfriend."

"And where is he from?"

Michal shrugged her shoulders. "From another village nearby, I think."

"A *Catholic* village?"

"I don't know," Michal admitted.

"In our village we are all Calvinists. The village is built on a small island. Since I came away, they tell me there is now a causeway joining the village to the mainland, but it wasn't so in my day. We never left the village. We all knew each other and we lived good, respectable lives, quite unlike those Catholics, who turn every Sunday into a day of amusements and pleasure and despise us for our virtues! To think that girl from my village might marry someone from outside! It's unthinkable!"

"Times change," Michal tried to explain gently. "Marika came to school in England. It's all quite different now."

"Which is why you came in her stead?"

"I came to see and work with the jewels of Sri Lanka, and to see Marika wed, not to marry a husband sight unseen, thank you very much!"

"Hoity-toity with it! You came here at Hendrik's expense, didn't you? He's hardly likely to pay for you to go away again."

"I still won't marry him!" Michal maintained firmly.

"We'll see. He would have been better off with a good girl from my own village, not some flighty wench no-one has ever heard of. But Hendrik says you look healthy enough to produce well-made children, so we'll have to learn to put up with you."

Michal was so angry she could hardly speak. "Hendrik knows I'll pay him back for any money he's expended on my behalf—with interest, if that's the way he wants it!"

Tante Willy was unimpressed. "What were your parents thinking of, letting you come all this way by yourself if you didn't have marriage in mind?"

"My parents are dead."

"No brothers or sisters?"

"No. I'm an only child."

"Ah, now we have it! You thought you'd cash in on Marika's good fortune and marry her burgher yourself! You could do worse. They make strong husbands. I should know. I had one myself!"

"I don't want a strong husband," Michal said with feeling. "Marika always said the people in her village regarded marriage as a business venture, and I never believed her, but I do now! I find it an outrageous idea to assess your future partner in life in terms of money!"

Tante Willy laughed scornfully. "How do you plan to pay Hendrik back for his generosity if you don't marry him?" she asked.

"I make and sell jewellery of my own design."

"It'll take you years!"

Michal hoped not! She gritted her teeth. "If it takes years—"

"Don't be so touchy, child! It's true you weren't chosen by the church elders for Hendrik, but he won't hold that against you. They should have done a better job when they had the chance." Tante Willy sniffed. "Things have obviously changed over there since I was a girl."

"Tell me about your village," Michal encouraged her.

"Haven't you ever seen it for yourself?" Tante Willy was surprised. "I remember it with increasing nostalgia. Sometimes I even long for a taste of the wester, the wind that cuts through one's garments like a knife. The houses are all painted green—most of them are wooden—and are as clean as a new pin. My people still wear their national costume and are proud of it. Our customs don't change from day to day. We had the church to keep us in line and the knowledge that our neighbours were always watching us—not unkindly, you understand, but to make sure no harm came to us. Until I was sent out here to be married, I'd never even slept in a proper bed. In our houses they are closed away in box-like cupboards. Ah, what I would give to be young again and be living there again!"

"Marika hated it," Michal offered. "She felt closed in and was in a constant state of rebellion whenever she went home. She may be happier with her Joost; at least she loves him."

"Does she?" Tante Willy snorted. "More likely she thought she'd have her fun before she settled down with Hendrik. She wouldn't have seen you as any danger to her plans."

"Why not?" Michal found herself asking.

"You haven't any money to recommend you to a solid citizen like Hendrik van der Aa. Any members of his family she will know are all as close-fisted as undertakers!"

"How do **you** know?" Michal demanded, resenting the aspersion on her friend.

"I was the same at her age. It's living out here that's made me aware of the dangers of copper-coloured hair and a figure to match. As a girl, I would have backed my money any time as the greater attraction for any right-thinking Hollander. It's taken me years to discover there are other things in life."

Michal was glad of the opportunity to turn the conversation away from herself. "You're lucky to have your daughter-in-law and grandson. I met Saman before breakfast. He's a charming boy."

"Foreigners, both of them!" Tante Willy said caustically. "I wouldn't have allowed it, but Hendrik overruled me. Hendrik's worth ten of my son any day. His son won't prefer a saffron robe to his father's business. A saffron robe! Do you know why they wear them? They're the shrouds from the dead. They wash them, of course, and sterilise them by boiling them with saffron, which gives them their colour, but that's what they are. Doesn't it make you shiver to think of it?"

"Not really," Michal denied. "They're a beautiful colour."

Tante Willy grinned broadly, looking suddenly very like her nephew. "If you think that, you silly child, you'd better stay and forget all that nonsense about your finer feelings and your needs to fall in love with the man you marry. Hendrik said you'd do very well—and I'm beginning to agree with him."

Tante Willy was carried out onto the verandah for tea.

"It makes a change of scene," she explained to Michal, "and it doesn't make much trouble. Belle and I can manage the outward journey between us, and Hendrik usually carries me back to my room after dinner."

"While I'm here I can help you, too," Michal offered.

The old lady's eyes snapped with amusement. "While you're here," she agreed. She obviously thought Michal would be there for life.

Saman joined them for tea. He treated his grandmother with an indulgent caution that amused Michal almost as much as it irritated Tante Willy. It was strange how one small boy could somehow seem to be older than either of them. He sat cross-legged on the floor, his expression solemn, and listened to their conversation with an air of total indifference. Only once did he speak, and then it was to his grandmother.

"You're worrying about nothing, madam," he said, smiling to himself. "Mr. Hendrik doesn't mind that Miss Michal doesn't come from your village. He'll enjoy having an English wife."

It was Michal who answered him. "Now, see here, young man, I have no intention of marrying your cousin. Nothing would induce me, either! This is one English girl who plans to marry one of her own countrymen, not a foreigner full of funny ideas."

The boy laughed. "Mr. Hendrik may change your mind," he warned her.

Michal's mouth closed into a stubborn line. "That's what you think!" she retorted. "I haven't found anything much to admire here yet!"

Tante Willy gave Michal a pained look. "Your parents should have taught you to be less free with your tongue," she reproved her. "Why don't you go and cool down your temper in the sea for a while? Saman and I can manage very well without you."

Michal burnt with humiliation. She had spent her whole life "minding her tongue," it seemed to her, for her elderly parents had disliked modern manners as much as they had disliked modern slang. Michal stood up, annoyed to find her knees were trembling, and went proudly to her room without a backwards glance. Tante Willy was a disappointment to her. She had hoped she would prove an ally against Hendrik's jade-green eyes and broad shoulders, a counterweight to the hollow feeling she got inside every time she thought of him. She shrugged her shoulders, resigning herself to being as alone as she always had been. All teen-agers had crushes on handsome men, she reassured herself. The only thing that was wrong with her was that she was a late developer. As soon as she got back to England, she would laugh at the memory of the effect his un-doubted masculinity had had on her. It was a temporary thing, meaning nothing, and she had other things to worry about. Somehow or other, she had to raise the money for her fare home. If she put all her energies into that, she wouldn't have time to moon over Hendrik van der Aa.

By the time she had pulled on her one-piece bathing suit, Michal was quite excited by the idea of going for a swim. She had never been allowed to swim in the sea as a child. At school she had been taken to the nearest swimming baths and had been taught the rudiments of how to propel herself through the water. Her friends had been taken to the seaside for holidays by their parents; hers had frowned on all such frivolities. Year after year, Michal had been taken to the cathedral city where her parents had spent their honeymoon. The hotel had smelt stale and musty, and so had most of the other guests, all of them middle-aged and with quite different interests from her own. They, like her parents, had their meals cooked for them and the housework done by someone other than themselves. They had wanted nothing else, and it had never occurred to them that Michal was bored stiff and had longed to fend for herself somewhere far away and romantic. In that sense Sri Lanka was proving the answer to a dream that was almost as old as she was.

Somehow, it added to her pleasure to put off the moment when she actually set foot on the coconut-fringed sands that stretched in both directions for as far as she could see. She could have hugged herself with glee to think that this was the Indian Ocean that was just outside her door.

To get to the beach she had had to walk a short distance down the road, past the village temple with its dazzling white dagoba, its dome surmounted by an aluminium painted top that caught the evening sun and was, momentarily, turned to pure gold. The entrance to the temple was guarded by the representations of two horrific gods, one of them with six faces and twelve arms, and the other riding on an unlikely looking goose. Michal was sorry that she didn't know more about the Hindu gods, but she imagined they had been brought to Sri Lanka by the many Tamil invaders who had crossed the narrow sea from South India.

It was almost immediately darker than she had allowed for. The sun, a great orange ball of light, was already bronzing the western sky as it fell inexorably behind the distant horizon. The villagers were lighting their lamps and the birds were winging their way home to their chosen night perches. The crows, as always, were the most vocal of them all, their harsh voices ringing through the evening air.

Even while she was telling herself to hurry, Michal lingered by the temple for a few minutes more. There was a tree in the courtyard, completely surrounded by a brick wall, and here and there, flags of cloth had been tied to its branches.

"I was told I'd find you here," Hendrik said at Michal's elbow. "That's a bo tree, a holy tree, because Buddha was sitting under a bo tree when he was enlightened. A branch of his tree was brought to Ceylon by the daughter of the Indian Emperor Asoka. Her brother brought the Buddhist message, and she the tree. The actual tree, the sapling taken from the Buddha's, is at Anuradhapura. It's reckoned to be the oldest living tree in the world."

"But this one is only a relation of that tree?"

"It's the same species," he agreed.

As he spoke a woman came into the courtyard, a number of coconut-oil lamps in her hands that she spread out beneath the tree, lighting them one by one. When she had finished, she went down on her knees and prostrated herself before the tree, the flames of her lamps flickering like so many glow-worms about her.

Michal blinked, concentrating hard on the beauty of the moment. If she didn't, she would have to come face to face with the alarming sensations Hendrik's mere presence could induce inside her. She felt weak in the middle and was horribly conscious that he had as few clothes on as she had herself. Did he intend to swim, also? She knew as surely as night followed day that he would be a magnificent swimmer. He was built for such pursuits, with his wide, strong shoulders and narrow hips.

He frowned at her. "If you walk through the village in daylight clad in nothing but your bathing suit, you'll cause a riot," he criticized her.

"I have a robe with me," she excused herself. "I took it off because I was hot, and it isn't as though there's anyone round to see me."

"There's me," he said.

A wave of heat passed through her at the look in his eyes. "You're wearing less than I am," Michal said flatly.

"I'm a man," Hendrik retorted. "The women here are more circumspect."

As if she needed his gender pointed out to her, she

thought darkly. She wished she could find something crushing to say to him, something that would upset that cool, arrogant confidence of his as surely as the assessing look in his eyes tied knots in her stomach.

"I'm not wearing a bikini, exactly!" she protested with spirit.

"No," he agreed.

"Well, then?"

A small smile curved his generous, sensual mouth. "A bikini would hardly be more revealing." He took her robe from her and put it round her shoulders. "If you want to go back to England, *meisje,* you should remember your namesake. It was David's other wife, Bathsheba, who tempted the king by bathing naked on her rooftop."

Her skin burned at the contact of his fingers. "David wanted to be tempted!"

His lips came within an inch of hers. "I am not averse to being tempted, either, little one. Do you want to swim, or not? Did anyone tell you to be careful of the undertow? This isn't a very dangerous beach, but don't go in deeper than your waist, or you may find yourself in difficulties. It's better that you shouldn't go in alone at all."

"I prefer to swim by myself," she informed him curtly.

He tapped her cheek with two fingers, almost stroking her skin as he did so. "You'll grow used to having me beside you in time." His eyes narrowed against the last of the light. "Have you always done everything alone?" he asked.

She pushed his hand away. "My parents were too old to want the company of a child." She bit her lip, finding that too revealing an answer. "I've always had plenty of friends my own age," she went on quickly, "but when I have children, I'd like to be young enough to enjoy doing things with them."

"I dare say that can be arranged," Hendrik said dryly.

She stepped away from him. "I'm in my middle twenties now, and I haven't met anyone I want to marry," she retorted with quiet emphasis.

He laughed, catching her by the wrist. "Anything can happen in Sri Lanka," he mocked her. "The Arabs used to call the island Serendip, from which comes our word 'serendipity,' the pleasure of making surprising discoveries—and all of them nice ones!"

To her relief, he let her go, striding across the sand with firm, deliberate steps until the water was deep enough for him to dive under the oncoming waves, his almost-white hair darkening dramatically as soon as it was wet enough for him to slick it back out of his eyes.

She followed him more slowly and found the water delightfully warm, with sudden eddies of a cooler current reminding her of his warning about getting out of her depth. She swam until she was tired, coming slowly out of the water, as if she were reluctant to leave the comfort it gave her.

He was sitting on the beach watching her every movement, and she took her time flicking her chestnut hair out of her eyes as an excuse for not joining him. The moon was shining over the sea and gave enough light for her to be able to see him clearly. The characteristic angle of his head annoyed her, because even though he was seated and she was standing up, he could still manage to look down his nose at her. She turned her back on him and wrung out her hair with an energy it hardly deserved.

"Come and sit down," Hendrik invited her, patting the fine sand beside him.

"I'd rather stand!"

His eyes flashed in the moonlight. "Afraid?"

She was as scornful as he. "Of you? Never!"

He sprang to his feet and she winced away from him, tensing her muscles, preparatory to taking to her heels.

"No?" He took the lapel of her swiftly donned robe and wiped a trickle of water away from her face. "Perhaps you should be—that is, if you are really serious about going back to England—"

She dug her toes into the sand, hoping he couldn't hear the thunder of her unruly heartbeat.

"What woman could fear a man who'd allow some elderly men in another country to choose his wife for him? A real man does his own courting!"

"You know so many?" he pressed her.

"A few!" Her lips felt unnaturally stiff as she uttered the lie.

"But you have never been close friends with any of them," he said certainly. "I think you're not nearly as experienced as you'd have me believe." He put an arm about her waist and pulled her close. "Are you cold?" Hendrik asked her.

Michal pulled away from him, refusing to let him know that it was his touch that was making her tremble, but he refused to let her go. Instead, he began to dry her through her robe.

"Don't!" she gasped.

His eyes narrowed. "Because you like it too well?" His hands were stilled, but she made no effort to move. It was as if her limbs were paralysed by the strength of the desire that shot through her.

"Let me go!" she gasped fiercely.

"Why? I hope to persuade you that this is a very good reason for your staying here with me. I want you, Michal Brent, and, with a little persuasion, you're going to want me, too." She could see the whiteness of his teeth and knew he was laughing at her. "You'll soon forget those other men of yours when I hold you in my arms."

She would have liked to have proved him wrong, but the rebellion his words induced disintegrated into a warm, delicious bubble of happiness as his lips came into contact with hers. She was changed into a stranger she never would have recognised as herself. She had no hesitation in rubbing her fingers against his bare chest, moving up to his neck and the damp hair that curled into the nape of his neck. Her mouth opened to his without protest as she clung to him more closely still. For a long, long moment there was only the sea, the sand, the moonlight, and the hard feel of his muscles as he held her helpless against him. This was a kiss like none other she had ever experienced, and she never wanted it to end.

Chapter Four

Hendrik released her, rolling away from her with a smothered exclamation. Michal lay back on the sand, wondering at the aching need she had felt for him a moment earlier. That need was only just beginning to drain away, leaving her weak and frightened of the strength of her own unexpected passion.

"Don't feel badly," Hendrik advised her kindly. "It happens to all of us sooner or later."

"But I know nothing about you!"

He pulled her robe up over her shoulders, brushing the loose sand from her neck. He was remote and matter-of-fact, but still overwhelmingly male and exciting to her. She was glad that he, at least, was in control of himself and the situation, because in her present mangled state, she couldn't imagine herself making much of anything, least of all of her own hectic emotions.

"You know all you need to know. Haven't you heard the saying that it's better to marry than to burn?"

She sat up. "I may have wanted to kiss you and have you kiss me *then,* but it won't happen again. I won't let it!"

She could feel his amusement and resented it. "You'll get used to it," he said gruffly. He pushed her back against the sand, stroking her cheek with a thoughtful finger. She was ashamed of the heat he would find in her face and tried to avoid his touch, even while this other, new person inside her welcomed every contact between them with a thoroughness she found shocking and totally irresponsible.

"I won't have time to get used to it! The sooner I go back to England, the better! I'm not the person you wanted to have for your wife, and a few kisses—that one might share with anyone!—won't change that!"

"My dear girl—"

"I'm not your dear *anything!*"

"No? I followed you down to the beach because I wanted to kiss you and find out if you might not like kissing me, too. A marriage would be a dull thing without that spark to keep it alive."

Her thoughts whirled in tune to the breathless sensation in her chest. "I won't marry without love," she reiterated stubbornly. "And *that* isn't love!"

"Words, empty words. Would you rather I kept you here without marriage?"

She stared at him in the darkness, trying to decide

if he meant what she thought he meant. He was good to look at. She couldn't imagine what it had been like before she had seen those jade-green eyes, touched him, and had her nostrils filled with the male scent of him. She must have been empty, indeed. She was tempted to move closer to him and leave the consequences to look after themselves, but some remnant of sanity prevented her. His kisses might have turned her theories on love upside down and inside out, but she wasn't silly enough to think that anything comparable had overtaken him. He had enjoyed kissing her—as he would have enjoyed caressing any attractive female who was unwise enough to come within his orbit.

"Sometime," Michal told him, "someone is going to take you seriously when you say something like that, but it won't be me. It wasn't my fault that Marika didn't come, and I don't see why I should suffer for it. You'll have to find someone else! I have other and better things to do!"

Hendrik's hands tightened on her arms and she could feel his warm breath against her mouth. "Is there someone back in England?"

There was a rough edge to his voice that disturbed her. Was this the way out she ought to take? She tried to summon up the strength to lie, and to lie convincingly enough to make the burgher let her go.

She felt frozen inside. "No."

"Then why not marry me?" His lips touched hers, warming the chill round her heart. His mouth was gentle, even tender, but his voice had that same warning edge to it that told her he meant to have his own way, whatever she had to say about it. "With your upbringing, I took it you'd prefer a ring on your finger before you shared a man's bed and board—"

Michal wrenched herself free. "You can't make me do anything I don't want to!" she stormed.

Hendrik came lightly to his feet with all the smoothness of a large cat. Michal shivered. How different it would have been if she had been the love of his life. But it was foolish to think like that. All he wanted was a wife, and any woman would do for that—first Marika, now herself; he wasn't at all particular.

"I won't let you go," he ground out.

"Why not? Tante Willy and her village will soon find someone else for you to marry. You don't need me—"

"I want you!"

"Then want must be your master!" Michal flashed back at him.

Hendrik's teeth shone in the moonlight, and she knew he was smiling. "Are you sure it won't be yours?" he retorted. The warning edge was gone, and his voice was as deep and gentle as warm syrup.

"What d'you mean?" she demanded unwisely.

"This," he said simply. He gathered her firmly into his arms, the weight of his hard body subduing hers with a ruthlessness that frightened her almost as much as it delighted her. His kisses demanded a response she could not deny. It was better even than it had been before as his hands confirmed her shape through the thin cloth of her swimming suit. She felt no shame at all, only a glorious weakening of her

61

resolve to resist him. Whatever he wanted, she wanted it, too, with an intensity that blinded her to the dangers of her situation.

"Are you going to marry me, little Miss Brent?"

The words came to her from far off. She struggled to concentrate on them, but they didn't seem to mean anything.

"What?" she said, frowning at the interruption.

"I asked if you wanted to marry me."

Despair filled her. How could she marry him, knowing he had none of the more tender feelings for her that she had hoped to have from her husband?

"Do I have to?" she groaned.

"No, you don't have to. I could keep you here as my mistress. Who would know?"

"I would," Michal said sadly.

"I think you would be happier as a married woman," Hendrik murmured against her lips. "Say yes, Michal!"

She jackknifed away from him. "Yes, yes, *yes!*" she almost shouted at him.

"You won't regret it," was all he said.

He sounded complacent and very, very sure of himself. With trembling hands, she covered herself from his view and the romantic light from the moon. The sand that clung to her skin rubbed painfully as she adjusted her robe back into position. She was lucky he hadn't torn it, as surely as he'd torn up her dreams, taking her compliance in this unromantic marriage for granted and offering her nothing in return. Yet, she didn't want to belong to *him*, not without love and without hope. What was to become of her?

She buried her fingers in the sand, seeking she knew not what. "I'm not ready to marry anyone! You'll have to give me time to get used to the idea."

"What makes you think it'll get any better?" he asked her. "All brides have pre-wedding nerves."

She hunched up her shoulders. "I always thought I'd be head-over-heels in love when I got married—and that my husband would love me!"

His hand covered hers, his fingers meeting hers in the sand. "There's no need for you to upset yourself, *mijne liefde*. What would life hold for you in England? A young girl on her own? Marika was doing you a favour to send you in her stead."

Michal sniffed. She didn't want him to know she was close to tears; it seemed so poor-spirited to cry. It wasn't the kind of thing a strong-minded English girl would do under any circumstances.

"I must have time," Michal said again.

"A day or two," Hendrik agreed in a matter-of-fact tone. "I went to Galle this afternoon and made the necessary arrangements. There are some jewellers there who you'll want to see. We'll visit them to-morrow and buy the ring at the same time. The church is in the old Dutch fort, as Dutch in character as any of those back home—"

"I'm not Dutch!"

"Tante Willy wouldn't approve of anything else. You'll marry me there, Michal, the day after to-morrow. As for the rest, I'm prepared to wait until you're ready for that."

He sounded as though he didn't think he'd have to wait long. She'd given him no reason to think so, after all.

Her mouth twisted into a wry smile. "It isn't what you're thinking," Michal said. "I'm not afraid to make love with you, only I think there ought to be more than lust as a reason for going to bed with any man."

"Words, my dear. You won't know the difference when I make you mine. I'm not like the inexperienced boys you've known up to now. I'm a man, and I know enough to give you more pleasure than you ever would have had with them."

The burghers make strong husbands. Hadn't Tante Willy told her that? But did they make loving husbands? She doubted if Hendrik van der Aa knew what the word meant.

She sighed, wriggling her fingers away from his. "I doubt if Tante Willy found much pleasure in marriage," Michal murmured.

"But you will," Hendrik said certainly. His fingers tightened on hers. "Won't you, Michal?"

"I need time!" she said again.

"Very well. Take your time!" he shot back at her. He leaned forward unexpectedly and kissed her on the cheek. "But don't take too long, because I mean to have a wife, a woman in my bed, and children in due time, and I don't mean to wait forever for them!" He stood up, pulling her up beside him. "How long is it going to take to convince you it isn't time you want, but a man to give a purpose to your life? We've both been lonely long enough."

Michal's heart missed a beat. What did he know of loneliness? she wondered. What did he know of that aching need to share a moment with someone other than an aged parent or a passing acquaintance?

The coconut lamps were still burning under the bo tree. They looked extraordinarily pretty, ranged along the wall round the tree. Michal paused and looked at them, her eyes blurring with tears. They weren't the only flames that had been lit that night, but those others were still something of a mystery to her. They might warm her, or they might burn her, but she doubted they would ever ignite a love that would bind Hendrik to her for the rest of their lives. She would have to make do, once again, with what was offered to her, but just this once it would have meant everything to her to have come first with someone, to have been of more importance to him than anyone else in the world, particularly if that someone should be Hendrik van der Aa.

The village boasted only a tiny sub-post office. Michal, who had some difficulty in getting away by herself, entered it with relief.

"I want to send a telegram to the Netherlands," she told the man in charge.

"An international telegram?"

"Yes. To Holland."

A lengthy search produced a few telegram forms from another era, with the symbols of the British Colonial Government stamped firmly on the top.

"These are internal telegrams," Michal pointed out.

"Telegram forms," the counter clerk growled firmly. "You want to send a telegram?"

"To Europe," Michal confirmed.

"Excuse me, madam. You write your message

here." The clerk pointed to one of his faded forms. "You have a pen?"

Michal accepted a blunt pencil he found in a drawer and wrote down her message where he had indicated:

HENDRIK MARRYING ME, INSTEAD. HELP. MICHAL.

She added the address with a sinking heart, convinced that Marika would never receive the telegram. The Dutch girl was her last line of defence. After a sleepless night, Michal had convinced herself that Marika would be as outraged as she was at her friend being forced into a marriage she didn't want. Marika had managed to extricate herself from the arrangement, preferring to stay with her Joost and tricking Michal into going in her stead. Now, surely, wouldn't she do something to protect her hapless victim?

Knowing Marika, Michal thought it unlikely that the Dutch girl would do anything. What could she do, after all? Marika had never been known to take an interest in anything which didn't directly affect herself. Michal's best hope was that Marika would be indignant that Hendrik had found her friend a fitting substitute for herself. She had never liked competition, not even when the prize was of no further interest to her.

Stepping outside into the hot sun again, Michal began to wish she hadn't come. She wouldn't have if Tante Willy hadn't put it into her head that she was stealing something valuable from Marika by marrying Hendrik in her place. Tante Willy had meant that the van der Aas were a good catch financially, which wasn't of any great importance to Michal. But in the night it came to her that if Marika were ever to see Hendrik for herself, she would be as angry as only Marika could be that she had fallen for Joost, instead.

Marika had to be warned, and how else could Michal tell her what was happening, except by sending her a telegram? The worst of it was that now she felt she was somehow betraying Hendrik by going behind his back.

Tante Willy had noticed at once the bruised look Michal had presented at dinner the night before.

"You look exhausted, girl!" she had declared. "Give her a drink, Hendrik. She looks as though she could do with one."

"Have you tried arrack before?" he had asked her.

She had never even heard of it. "I'll try anything once," she had claimed. What was a drink after what she had already been through?

Hendrik had mixed the drink for her, telling her that arrack was made from the flower of the coconut palm. With a thoughtful look at her, he had added a double quantity of passion-fruit cordial and had added several cubes of ice.

"If it goes to your head, there are several of us willing to put you to bed," Hendrik had assured her, with a look to intimate that her courage had deserted her. The very thought of Hendrik putting her to bed had sent quivers through her body. She had to concentrate hard on the task of tasting the drink without having the glass clatter against her teeth, betraying her shattered nerves to them all.

She had liked the drink itself, and she had felt very much better for it. She would have liked another, but Hendrik, his green eyes mildly amused, had said, "I think not, *meisje*. You'll have to get your kicks another way."

"I'm not looking for kicks," Michal said hotly.

His eyebrows had shot upwards, and his eyes had shone as green as grass. "Perhaps you've already had enough for tonight," he had drawled, and both he and Tante Willy had laughed out loud.

That hadn't meant that Tante Willy had approved of Hendrik's announcement at dinner that he meant to marry Michal in her friend's stead. The Dutch woman had sniffed, glaring at them both across the table.

"What's the hurry? Marika will come in her own time, as soon as she tires of this unsuitable young man who's caught her eye. What do we know of this other one?"

Hendrik's mouth had tightened into a thin line. "Michal is here; Marika isn't."

Tante Willy had sniffed again. "Marika comes from the same village as we do. She shares our values. If you have any sense, you'll pay this girl to go home and wait for the bride who was chosen for you. At the very least, you should tell Marika what you mean to do and give her a chance to accept her fate gracefully."

"Marika has chosen someone else!"

Michal had heard the pain in Hendrik's voice. It had ripped through her, evoking a new emotion she had never known before. Belatedly, she recognised it as jealousy. Marika was the girl he wanted to marry, even though he knew her only through her photographs, and who could be surprised at that? Marika wasn't beautiful, but she had a style and distinction that Michal would never have in a hundred years.

"Has she?" Tante Willy asked, enjoying the trouble she was making. "She'd come like a shot if she thought there was any danger of losing you to anyone else."

"She's marrying Joost," Michal protested. "At least, I think she is," she amended. "They have some . . . some arrangement or other." Her voice faded away in a tired whisper as her stomach contracted into a knot of pain. "I agree. She ought to be told," Michal added faintly.

"It's too late," Hendrik retorted grimly. "She sent you in her stead, and she can take the consequences."

"What consequences?" Michal asked, bewildered.

It was Tante Willy who answered her. "The van der Aas are one of the richest families in the East," she said dryly. "And the Dutch are a practical people. Joost won't be nearly such an attractive proposition to Marika's family."

"But if she's in love with him . . . ?"

Tante Willy neighed with laughter. "Romantic dreams are all very well for a few years, but good marriages last a lifetime. If you ask me, Joost won't last five minutes! I take it he hasn't sixpence to call his own?''

"I really don't know," Michal said with dignity. She found all this talk of possessions distasteful. She wouldn't have cared if Hendrik hadn't a single penny in the world—and she was sure that Marika wouldn't care, either! Well, she was almost sure. And then, quite suddenly, she wasn't sure at all! Marika would have to be warned about Hendrik's defection, just in case, and she, Michal, would have to be the one to do it.

How to tell Marika of Hendrik's plans for herself exercised her mind throughout the sleepless night that followed. The idea of sending a telegram had come with the dawn—and now she had done it. What she wouldn't admit to herself, and wouldn't have dreamed of admitting to anyone else, was the curious sensation of relief she felt that it seemed highly unlikely the telegram would ever be sent. Not only had it been sent on the wrong form, but it had been ridiculously cheap, far too cheap for any telegram to travel all the way to Europe! It was a comforting thought, and one she hugged to her as she sauntered down the one street the village boasted, peering curiously into the tiny shops, made of wood and palm leaves, and which were full of colourful lengths of locally made cloth, fish, vegetables, and more kinds of fruit than Michal had ever seen before in her life.

A car drew up beside her. She paid it no attention, imagining it had stopped for somebody else, until she realised that it was Hendrik who was at the wheel and that he was trying to attract her attention.

"I'm off to Galle. Want to come with me?" he shouted across the crowd to her.

The jade-green eyes met hers with a challenge in their depths that brought a prickle of anticipation running up and down her spine.

"What's at Galle that isn't here?" Michal retorted. *Besides a Dutch church in a old Dutch fort,* she added to herself.

"Come and find out!" Hendrik invited her.

She pushed her way through the good-humoured crowd, avoiding the dogs that were less easily diverted from their chosen paths. The sight of Hendrik was as welcome as the flowers in spring back home. It made her want to cry out with longing. Instead, she leaned against his open window.

"Isn't that where they have the jewellers' shops?"

He nodded. "The tears of Adam and Eve, which they shed when they were banished from Paradise, fell on the earth as sapphires, tourmalines, garnets, quartz, spinel, and zircons. That's why Ceylon is thought to have been Sindbad's valley of diamonds. It's mostly his countrymen who buy and sell the stones today. Are you coming?"

Her fingers tightened on the open window. "Are you sure you want me with you?"

"Get in, Michal!"

She went round the car and slithered into the seat beside him. "You don't have to entertain me as well as . . . everything else!" she said in a rush.

He turned towards her with a purposeful air.

"Leave the mischief-making to Tante Willy, Michal." He surveyed her guilty face with narrowing eyes. "What have you been up to?"

She hoped he would think the blush in her cheeks was caused by the hot sun. "I? Nothing? What could *I* possibly do?"

Hendrik put his hand over hers. "I won't let you go!" There was no tenderness in the statement, nothing but a gritty determination that made Michal wonder why marriage should be so important to him. If he were as rich as Tante Willy had suggested, why didn't he take time off to go to Europe to find a wife for himself?

"You know nothing about me, as Tante Willy keeps pointing out," Michal reminded him wryly. "You'd be much better off helping me to buy a few jewels so that I can earn my fare home by means of the work I know best. I'm a very good jewellery designer!"

"I hope so," he said.

She eyed him suspiciously. "Isn't that rather inconsistent of you?" she demanded.

His expression was bland. "I don't think so. I had it in mind to give you some pleasure, as a matter of fact. At Galle there are several gem factories. I thought we'd visit one of them."

Michal wondered why she felt as if her whole world was falling about her ears. "You've changed your mind!" she accused him. "You're going to let me earn my fare home, after all?"

A muscle jerked in Hendrik's cheek, but there was no other clue as to what he was thinking. She clenched her fists in her lap, trying to feel a little joy in her heart at the thought of going home.

"No," he said at last, "I haven't changed my mind. I just thought you might like to design your own engagement ring?"

"An *engagement* ring?" Michal repeated stupidly.

Hendrik ran a finger down her reddened cheek, then turned his attention back to his driving.

"It is customary when two people bind themselves to marry each other." He slanted a smile at her.

"But we haven't—"

"Oh, yes, we have!" he said.

Chapter Five

It seemed too good to be true. Michal would have the gems and the means to make something of them. All she had to do was find some outlet whereby she could sell the ring and buy her ticket back to England. It wasn't fighting fairly, of course, but then she didn't consider Hendrik had treated her fairly, either. And she would repay him every penny of the money, if it took her a lifetime of hard work to do it. He wouldn't be the loser in any way. In fact, he would probably be relieved in the end to be so easily rid of her. If Tante Willy was right, Marika would soon be there to comfort him, and if Michal didn't think such material considerations were a proper basis for marriage, it was really none of her business.

Michal was just dreaming of how nice it would be if she could find herself in control of events for once and have Hendrik van der Aa at her mercy, instead of the other way round, when she caught sight of a man and a baby elephant walking along the side of the road.

"Oh, where are they going?" Michal asked, leaping up and down in her excitement. "Please stop for a moment. I've never seen a real working elephant before."

"That one's too young to work," Hendrik pointed out.

"But it will be a working elephant!"

Obligingly, he pulled onto the side of the road and got out of the car, calling a greeting to the baby elephant's keeper.

"He's being taken to his mother," Hendrik translated for Michal. "She's been out working since early morning, pulling out old coconut palms. Now her baby's being taken out to join her."

Michal played with the baby, allowing him to search her pockets for tidbits with his hairy trunk. "Surely they don't expect nursing mothers to work?" she exclaimed, a little indignant on the mother's behalf.

Hendrik smiled at the picture she made. "That young fellow is older than he looks. He's all of two years old. His mother was probably glad to get away from him for a while and wreak some havoc. She'll only be given light work at first, and all elephants enjoy pushing over trees."

He tossed a coin to the elephant's keeper and gestured to Michal to get back in the car. The elephant trotted off, waving its trunk in the air to get the first smell of its mother as they approached the coconut plantation where the mother had been working.

Michal stood and watched the elephant go, one hand on the open door of the car. She was as much aware of Hendrik's tall, strongly muscled frame as she was of the elephant, but she tried to pretend to herself that she wasn't, that he meant absolutely nothing to her and never would.

The bubble of complacency burst as he joined her on her side of the car, holding the door for her. The look in his eyes sent her scuttling into the car, her heart hammering. To her surprise, he didn't shut the door on her, as she had expected him to. He bent his head, almost following her into the car.

"Don't get any ideas about running out on your promise to me, Michal. I'll only follow you to England and bring you back!"

Her eyes opened wide as she presented him with a startled face. "You don't want me—" she began.

"I want to make love to you," he mocked her lightly.

"That's not enough."

"It will be!"

His lips met hers, his tongue fleetingly meeting hers, and then he had stepped back, shutting the door on her. A second later they were off again down the road towards Galle.

The yard was full of people working. Michal was delighted by the busy scene before her and turned to Hendrik to express her thanks to him for bringing her. The stern line to his jaw kept her silent, however. He must have been here many, many times before, and he probably had little interest in the proceedings of turning rough gems into polished jewellery of taste and charm. She bit her lip and turned back to the workshop. It wasn't at all like the one she had shared for a whilst back home.

There was no electricity; all the tools had to be turned by hand. The results achieved were not as fine as their automated counterparts, though they had their own charm, as had hand-turned pottery when compared with the factory-made product.

Excitement stirred Michal's blood as she recognised the various polishing devices and watched a young boy operate a wheel with his toes, using his nimble fingers to hold the rough stones against the polisher.

"What a marvellous place!" she exclaimed happily, still not looking in Hendrik's direction, in case he was still angry with her, though why he should be, she couldn't imagine. He couldn't have guessed her plans for the ring she was going to make.

The owner of the workshop came forwards to greet them. The light colour of his skin and the grey of his eyes betrayed his origins as much as the Muslim cap he was wearing. He looked very much as Sindbad must have looked many centuries before.

"Madam is a professional?" he suggested.

Michal warmed to him, giving him the details of her training and experience, eager to be back at work. She had missed the sight and smell of the jewels and the hot metals that were used to transform them into rings and brooches and other pieces.

The man knew as much about Hatton Gardens in London as she did herself. He asked if she knew the firm he normally dealt with and they spent a long time discussing the style of that firm, as compared to the one she had worked for.

"But now you don't work there anymore?" He smiled at her.

"No," Michal admitted. She had been about to tell him how Marika had persuaded her to give up her job to come to Sri Lanka with her, but she thought better of it. "I'm hoping to do free-lance work," she told him, instead. She gave him a wide-eyed smile. "Do I have any chance of selling my work?"

"Of course," he assured her easily, his eyes wandering across to the silent Hendrik. "It can be arranged. We have the best materials here for you to work with, and you have your own inside knowledge of the international market centred in London. It will only depend on your skill as a designer."

She nodded her head briskly. "I have a lot of ideas. No matter how good a stone is, it needs a good setting to show it off. I've seen good jewels marred by bad design and workmanship."

The man laughed softly. "Here, our local conventions govern our designs, especially as far as rings are concerned. We are very superstitious about all gems, especially those that are lucky for our date of birth. It's considered necessary for the stones to be in contact with the skin to be most effective. This limits much variety in the settings we use." His grey eyes twinkled at her. "Most people, if they haven't enough money to buy the right stone to bring them good luck, hire them from us, instead. Women in labour, men starting a new career, people preparing for marriage—they all need a lucky stone to keep the Evil One away."

Michal's laughter rang out. "Do you believe that?"

He acknowledged her question with a helpless gesture. "As a good Muslim I shouldn't, yet I wear my own birthstone, just the same." He held out his hand for her inspection. "We came here from Yemen in my grandfather's time, so Sri Lanka is home to me, and we've made most of the local customs our own."

Michal wondered how much of that same philosophy could be applied to Hendrik. How much was he Dutch, and how much Lankan? Not that it mattered, for both cultures were foreign to her, the Dutch less so, except as interpreted by Tante Willy and the elders of the old-fashioned Calvinist village from which she had come. Michal had no intention of staying long enough to find out how much their creed had affected Hendrik. He was Marika's business, not hers!

Hendrik came across the room to join them. His expression was still unyielding and slightly menacing, and Michal took a step away from him out of sheer nervousness. She sighed, wishing she could put him out of her mind as easily as he could put her out of his. Had she been too friendly with the Yemeni? Surely Hendrik couldn't be angry with her because of that.

"I brought my fiancée today to buy a suitable stone for her engagement ring," Hendrik told the man in a businesslike tone. "She'll make up the ring herself in a style that pleases her. May we see what you have?"

"Of course, sir."

"And any other stones you have," Michal added breathlessly, bringing all her courage to bear on the request. "I hope to buy a few and work on them for my old firm in London."

"You will have to consider the Customs tariffs," the merchant warned her. "The gems are cheap enough to buy here, but the taxes the governments take will make your prices less competitive by the time they arrive in England."

"I still mean to have a try," Michal said firmly. She cast Hendrik a covert look from beneath her lashes and was relieved to see he showed no sign of upsetting her plans for freedom. She relaxed visibly, feeling much more sure of herself.

"Have you enough money?" Hendrik asked her suddenly.

She flushed scarlet. "A bit. Not enough to pay my fare back to England, but I expected to earn enough by working while I was here. I'll pay you back every penny you've spent on me!"

He shook his head. "You'll keep what you can earn for pocket money. My wife won't have to work for a living."

"I'm not your wife!" she reminded him sharply.

"I have your promise, though, and that makes you my betrothed."

Betrothed was the sort of old-fashioned word her parents would have approved of, Michal thought. There was no doubt in her mind that they would both have approved thoroughly of Hendrik van der Aa, too, just as they would have approved of Tante Willy and her weird idea that all one needed to make a marriage work was more than one's share of this world's goods.

"You had Marika's word, and it didn't do you much good!" Michal retorted.

"I had her parents' word. Yours, you gave me in person."

The touch of asperity in his tone conjured up a vivid picture of how easily she had succumbed to his lovemaking. It would never happen like that again, she assured herself, but an uneasy shadow of that frightening stranger inside her made her keep her thoughts to herself.

Hendrik's brooding look softened as a reflective smile curved his sensual lips. "I shan't let you go," he said.

Michal told herself she had imagined the slight stress on the "you." She didn't matter to him one bit as a person, no more than Marika had. She meant nothing more to him than any other woman did, even if he did mean to marry her.

"They're ready for you to choose the stone for your ring. What would you like? A sapphire?"

"There are many cheaper stones," she felt obliged to point out. She supposed that he would pay for the stone for the engagement ring, and it would be embarrassing if it realised far more than she needed for her fare.

"I think Mrs. van der Aa should have the best the island can offer," he answered slowly. "Our Ceylon sapphires are the very best."

A tide of rebellion swept through Michal. An engagement ring ought to be something special to the couple concerned, an outward sign of the inward love they bore one another, not a financial transaction that meant nothing to either of them.

"I don't want a sapphire!"

"You don't care for blue?"

Blue sapphires were her absolute favourites to work with. "Blue can look cold," she said.

His eyes swept over her face. "Then we'll look at the ruby and pink sapphires first," Hendrik conceded. "We'll come back to these."

Michal waited for the merchant to turn away to fetch another tray. "Sapphires cost too much money!" she said in a fierce whisper. "I'd rather have something personal to me—that you might give me, anyway, as a . . . as a friend," she ended lamely.

"Relax. I'm not buying you with any ring, and I shan't expect anything from you in return. I'm not exactly a pauper; I can well afford to give my future wife the ring of her dreams!"

Which was only another way of putting it, she thought forlornly. It still sounded remarkably like a business transaction to her.

She bent her head over the tray, pretending to examine the stones in front of her, but actually unable to see them through the tears that had come rushing into her eyes.

"What do you do that brings you such riches?" Michal asked in a bantering tone that sounded so nearly normal she felt quite pleased with herself.

"Guess!" Hendrik invited her.

She tried to remember what had brought the Dutch to Ceylon in the first place, before the British had wrested the island from their control. Spices! That was it! she thought in triumph. Cinnamon. It had been cinnamon that had enticed first the Portuguese and then the Dutch to add Sri Lanka to their growing empires. Their rule had left a great deal to be desired, too, yet here was one of their descendents, comfortably installed in his adopted land, part of the fabric of the life of the modern island. It showed how closely entwined a people's history is with its present reality.

"Conquest and spices," she said.

"The latter, certainly. I'll show you my favourite spice garden on the way home, if you like? I buy and sell other things, but spices are still my major interest."

She accepted the offer gracefully, conscious that the gem merchant had come back to join them and to invite them to go into the room behind the factory that served as an office and a showroom. Here, he had laid out several trays for their inspection.

"It will be easier for you to make a choice when you see them all together," the merchant said in a businesslike tone. "These are the very best I have."

It was a magnificent collection. The different-coloured gems lay in rows on the velvet-lined trays, a great mass of radiant drops of light. Slowly, Michal examined them one by one, rejecting some, putting others aside for future consideration, mostly to be rejected in their turn and replaced by other, yet more perfect, jewels.

She was very much the professional now, commenting on the flaws that detracted from their value, and asking the questions that all jewellers asked when they were either buying or selling.

"All these gems are from the Ratnapura mines," the merchant told her. *"Ratna dvipa,* the island of gems." He left her to her own devices, sitting down on a chair to watch the proceedings from a distance.

"Did you know the four-hundred-carat 'Blue Belle' that adorns the British Crown came from Sri Lanka?"

Michal had known. She had seen it often when she had taken visitors to London to see the Crown Jewels in the Tower. "Are you going to claim it back?" she asked him.

He laughed. "Not that! Other things we would like to have in our own museums, but that is a better advertizement for our wares where it is!" He leaned forward, examining in his turn the jewels Michal had put aside. "You have good taste, madam. If you're going to live here, you must learn the Sinhala words for our gems: *nila; ratha; pushparaga; vairodi.* It will be my pleasure to teach you, and then you can buy directly from the mines."

"I'd love that!" Michal enthused. She frowned over the jewels she had placed to one side. "Some of these yellow sapphires are magnificent, but I can't like them all the same." She turned to Hendrik. "What do you think?"

He shrugged. "You're the expert! Why do some of the blue ones have that whitish sheen? Is that good or bad?"

She smiled up at him, her good humour completely restored by the pleasure of handling such beautiful stones. "Bad. It's called 'silk.' If you look at one of them through a jeweller's glass you can see for yourself the infinite little flaws that cause it. See? It isn't always bad, though. It depends on fashion, and one can't be too arbitrary about these things. Even the difference between precious and semi-precious stones changes with their scarcity value and what is in demand at the time. There's no such thing as intrinsic value in gems. Beauty is very much in the eye of the beholder!"

"Then I can buy you a sapphire, after all?"

Her cheeks were flushed with her pleasure in her task. Momentarily, she hesitated, and then she gave way with a rueful smile. "This one!" she breathed, placing a single blue sapphire in the centre of her palm. "It's the most perfect sapphire I've ever seen!"

Hendrik scarcely looked at it. "We're taking this one, Assif. Wrap it up, will you?"

The merchant smiled wryly at Michal. "It's a good choice. I have nothing better in my shop."

She smiled back at him in triumph. "Nothing!"

But her triumph gave way to anxiety when Hendrik and the merchant went out of her earshot to discuss the price and the amount of silver she would need to make a complementary setting for her choice. For a moment she thought of joining them, to tell Hendrik she had changed her mind and wanted something that would make less of a hole in his pocket. She would never be able to repay him the cost of such a fine jewel! However, the set of

Hendrik's shoulders told her that such a course would not be welcome, and she didn't have the courage to cross him in public.

So she turned her attention to the more rewarding task of choosing a few minor stones for her own purposes: some of the vari-coloured tourmalines; some stones from the corundum family—white, blue, violet, green, and ruby, all of them flawed, but lovely, all the same; and some pieces of spinel, topaz, and zircon.

Assif made no fuss about accepting her traveller's cheques. Of greater concern to her was the ridiculously low price he asked for the stones she had picked out. She wondered if Hendrik had already paid him most of the asking price, and she was sure of it when the merchant produced a lucky moonstone out of his drawer and threw it in with all the rest.

"It will bring you good fortune on your wedding night," Assif assured her, placing it with the other stones in a little woven coconut-leaf pouch. "It's very auspicious for romance, especially as it's a full moon to-morrow—the best time of all to marry!"

Only there was precious little romance about her marriage! Hers had nothing to do with love. It had only to do with Hendrik van der Aa needing an heir for his spice empire and her being the nearest nubile female round to secure his vision of the future. Not that she would be round for long, she comforted herself. She would sell the sapphire and be back in England long before the knot could be tied.

The moonstone was very pretty, though. Held up

to the light, it lived up to its name, having the same sheen as the full moon in a black velvet sky. She would keep it always, and she told Assif as much, her eyes still lingering on its pearly luster as she accepted a lemonade from his assistant's hand, knocking the straw right into the bottle, making it impossible to drink.

Amusement tugged at the corners of Hendrik's mouth. He took the bottle from her and retrieved the straw with a pair of tweezers that was lying on the desk where she had just finished signing her cheques.

"What will you do with your moonstone?" Hendrik asked her. "If you put it under your pillow, you may see your true love's face in it to-morrow."

That was something Michal didn't want in case it came true and the features she saw there were dark from the sun, with corn-coloured hair and eyes the colour of the flashing bee-eaters on the banks of the river. It was going to be hard enough to leave him as it was.

"Thank you for the sapphire, Hendrik," she said awkwardly.

His eyes were very bright and seemed to see right through her. "Guard it well, my disapproving Michal. The van der Aas regard marriage as an unbreakable bond—and I have your promise, remember?"

"You promised me all the time I needed," she whispered back. "Yet, you're hurrying me into having the wedding to-morrow. Why should I keep my word any better than you've kept yours?"

"I won't take anything from you that you don't want to give," he answered stiffly. "Can you say the same?"

Michal sucked uncomfortably at her straw. It was a real one, she noticed, and not one of the paper or plastic imitations she had known all her life. The sweat prickled between her shoulder blades and her clothes stuck to her, making her feel hotter than ever.

"Is it a guilty conscience that's given you those shadows under your eyes?"

She started. The heat in the room was unbearable. She longed to go outside, somewhere far away from Hendrik where she could nurse her distress in solitude.

"*My* conscience is clear!" Michal declared.

"I hope so," Hendrik mocked her. "We burghers take our vows very seriously—as you will find out."

She put her hand up to the collar of her dress and pulled at it. "I'm no burgher," she pointed out. "I'm not even Dutch!"

"A burgher's wife. We Dutch are a stubborn people and never let go of anything which we consider to be ours."

She was glad to be able to contradict him about that, at least. "The British took Ceylon away from you," she reminded him smugly. "*I'm* British!"

"I think not, *meisje,* but that reminds me of something I want to say to you before to-morrow. Shall we go out to the car?"

The car was like an oven, despite the fact that Hendrik had parked it in the shade of a tree. Michal helped him wind down all the windows, and together they sat on the burning front seat, stunned by the oppressive heat.

Hendrik fingered the steering wheel thoughtfully. "I promised you time, Michal, but I don't want you to think our marriage is a game of make-believe. I want a wife, and while you think you want high romance and a long and attentive courtship, that's the dream of a child. A grown woman needs other things from marriage as well, like security and the protection of a good man. We'll make a good life together."

"I only want love, not *things!*"

"Love is something which grows."

She shook her head at him. "You don't know what it means to love anyone," she accused him. "I don't want your goods and your protection. I don't want you!"

His eyes narrowed dangerously. "No?"

"No!"

"You wanted me on the beach, and to-morrow you'll want me again, just as I want you. You're a very attractive woman, Michal Brent. You won't find me a reluctant lover."

"Lover?" she repeated with contempt. "You'll never be my lover! The only thing you know about is physical desire and . . . and money!" She felt suddenly breathless and rather less sure of herself. If he were to take her in his arms and kiss her now, would she know the difference? "Anyway," she added unwisely, "I'm not going to stay round and find out!"

His hand curled about her chin, forcing her face to within an inch of his own. She could see the sheen of sweat on his forehead and the piercing green of his eyes.

"What do you mean by that?" Hendrik demanded.

Michal licked her lips. "I don't want to marry you! Why pick on me? Marika may have changed her mind by now, or the elders will send you somebody else, someone who won't mind a bloodless marriage of convenience—*your* convenience, without any consideration for her feelings at all!"

In the silence she could hear her own heart beating, or was it his? She put out a hand and laid it flat against his chest, grasping the opening of his shirt as if her life depended on it. The hair on his chest was rough against her fingers, sending a spark of electricity up her arm and turning her bones to molten wax.

His kiss still managed to take her by surprise. His tongue touched her lips and she was lost, drowning in the green of his eyes. She uttered a gasp of sheer ecstacy, clutching at his shirt more tightly than ever. His mouth explored hers with an arrogant mastery from which there was no escape. She wound her body closer against his, filling her senses with the feel and the male smell of him. How good it was to be close to him, to be overwhelmed by their mutual need for each other. But that was only on her side, she reminded herself. She was falling in love with this man, but that didn't mean he loved her.

She pulled away from him, brushing the tears out of her eyes with the back of her hand. He sat beside her for a long moment, watching her every movement with a hunger she understood all too well. She was hungry for the sight and touch of him, too.

"It won't be such an unequal marriage, after all," Hendrik said at last. "Will it? It may prove to be very *convenient* to us both." He gave her his slanting smile.

Michal said nothing at all. The sour taste of defeat was on her tongue, because she knew now she wasn't going to run away. She wasn't going to sell the sapphire, and she would probably never see England again. She was going to stay and marry Hendrik van der Aa, and she thought her heart would break with the knowledge of her own weakness as surely as he'd crushed the last of her fragile dreams for a loving future.

Chapter Six

Michal tried to tell herself that the headache was caused by the heat, but she knew it wasn't that at all. It was the realisation that she really was going to become Mrs. Hendrik van der Aa the next day, accompanied by the sinking feeling that afterwards she wouldn't be a person in her own right at all. She wouldn't even have a name of her own. The headache was no more than a cloud of depression brought on by this threatened anonymity, combined with the bleak knowledge that there was nobody in the whole world who would care on a personal level if she married Hendrik or not.

Only Marika might care. She wouldn't care about Michal's feelings in the matter, but she might care about losing Hendrik if he were as wealthy as everyone seemed to think.

She put her head back against the seat and closed her eyes.

"Tired?" Hendrik asked her.

The sympathy in his voice was almost too much for her. "I'm not used to the heat," she answered, excusing her weakness.

"It'll be cooler at the spice garden."

Michal hoped it would be. She hoped she'd feel better able to cope by then. "I'm sorry I cried all over you," she blurted out. Her throat felt too tight for the thread of voice to escape, but it seemed he had heard her, for he put out a reassuring hand and patted her on the knee.

"I *never* cry!" The untruth of this statement struck her with a rush, and she felt a strong urge to giggle. "Not in public, anyway," she amended. "I can't think what came over me."

"Every bride suffers from nerves on the eve of her wedding," Hendrik said calmly. His glance was a shade too arrogantly complacent for her comfort, and a surge of renewed spirit passed through her.

"Of course!" she agreed with obvious sarcasm. "Why didn't I think of that? It couldn't possibly be your fault, could it?"

"It could be, but it isn't," he replied positively. "Give it a rest, and allow yourself to enjoy your day out. You're a nice person to have round, because you do enjoy things—usually."

"Thank you very much!"

"Now what's the matter?" he asked, exasperated.

"Nothing. I just want to amount to something more than being an appendage for the rest of my life. Mrs. van der Aa sounds so foreign, and not like me at all!"

"Ah!"

"What's that supposed to mean?" Michal threw at him.

"Assif treated you as a professional in your own right. Coming from a Muslim, didn't that build up your confidence a bit?"

Michal sighed. "Muslims always have acknowledged that women are good at things—in their own sphere. What I want is something of my own! I shall trade under my own name, whatever you say!"

"Ah!" Hendrik said again.

"I'm not going to argue about it!" she said. "I must have something!"

"You haven't tried being Mrs. van der Aa yet," he pointed out.

"No," she agreed.

He shot a quick, comprehensive look at her flushed face. "It may not be as bad as you think. I can think of several compensations—"

"Like possessions!"

"Not unless you want to think of yourself as one of my possessions. I'd thought of a more equal relationship than that, but if that's what you want—"

She saw he had laid a trap for her, and she had been stupid enough to fall into it. She wouldn't make that mistake again. She would keep her doubts to herself and talk of other things. She would wait until she really knew what she wanted, and then she would take it, without any talk at all. His love might never be hers for the taking, but she thought she could make him like her, perhaps even have an affection for her. She knew he wanted her physically, and that was a good beginning. She would take the second-best he was offering her and make of it something beautiful for herself. She had to do that, she thought, or their life together wouldn't be worth living at all.

After that, she let her thoughts wander where they would, determined to put everything about tomorrow out of her mind. She began to plan the kind of setting she wanted to create for her sapphire engagement ring. After a few moments she forgot the purpose of the ring in her pleasure at solving the problem its design presented. She would make of it something heavy and old-fashioned looking, she thought. That would suit the atmosphere in the van der Aa household as much as it suited her own ideas about the important place marriage should have in anyone's life. They were ideas carefully instilled in her by her elderly parents, but ideas she had never seriously questioned, preferring to think that one day her husband would be the only lover she would ever want.

Would Hendrik van der Aa be that?

She caught herself up sharply, jolting forwards in her seat. His amused, questioning look made her wonder if he had read her thoughts. She certainly hoped not, but a blush of shame crept up her cheeks, to her dismay, and she thought he would have had to be a fool not to have known what she was thinking about.

She was sure of it a second later. "Penny for them?" he mocked her, solemnly producing a small coin from his pocket.

"I was thinking about my ring!" That was a safe enough topic, and one where she had the advantage, because she could produce an endless number of technicalities to confuse him if the going got rough.

Hendrik raised an eyebrow. "And what conclusions have you come to?"

Michal produced a small pad and a pencil from her purse and drew a few lines to show him the Georgian effect she had in mind.

"Like it?" she asked.

Hendrik glanced across at it. "It looks more like a man's ring. Won't it be too heavy for your finger?"

She inspected her hands carefully, shaking her head. "I don't think it'll be too much of a good thing. I like big rings."

He grasped her ring finger between two of his, slowing the car almost to a stop, glancing at the drawing again. She wriggled her hand and his hold tightened.

"You're right," he conceded suddenly, letting her go. "It'll accentuate the delicacy of your bones. You have small hands for your size."

"They're useful hands, rather than beautiful," she regretted. "I'd love to have long, slender fingers like Belle's."

He smiled slowly at her, his eyes very green. "Why is it women are never satisfied with the way they look?"

"For the same reason that men aren't, either!" she retorted, laughing. The strained atmosphere between them had gone, and with it went the last of her headache. "If the ring turns out as well as I expect it to, I could arrange to put it on display—"

He shook his head with decision. "You'll display it on your finger—and nowhere else!"

"It could be important to my career," she began to argue with him. "A few really fine pieces like that, and I could establish quite a reputation for myself."

His teeth showed briefly. "There'll be other pieces. Your ring is something private between the two of us. It's not for public display."

"I suppose it's your badge of ownership?" Michal said nastily.

"Isn't the wedding ring for that?" Hendrik countered smoothly.

"We didn't buy a wedding ring!" she reminded him sharply.

His smile grew wider. "I thought you'd want to make that, as well."

She was startled into returning the smile. It felt good to relax the muscles of her face, just as it felt good to lower her lashes and peer at him through their long length. She took in a quick breath and drew in her cheeks thoughtfully. She ought to know by now that it was dangerous to flirt with anyone of Hendrik's calibre. Yet, how easy it would be to give way to the delicious excitement she knew was to be found in his arms and not to care about anything else. It would be nice for once to be as uninhibited in her emotions as she was in her work, completely sure of herself and of the effects she wanted to achieve.

"Do you know how much work goes into making a ring?" she demanded.

"Enough to keep you out of trouble to-night!" He pushed a strand of copper hair away from her face, saying something in Dutch that she didn't understand.

"And then some! You expect miracles, Hendrik van der Aa!"

"I haven't been disappointed yet," he drawled.

Hendrik became a much more relaxed and charming person as he showed her round the spice garden. For long moments together she was able to forget the threat he posed to her integrity as a person, and to enjoy herself as she had not been able to do before in Ceylon. He even told her fascinating stories about the trade he obviously enjoyed as much as she enjoyed hers.

"It was Marco Polo who brought back to Europe the first rumours of strange 'dragons' from the East that could breathe fire into a man's mouth, leaving a sweet aftertaste that would have him panting for more. Pepper was the first favourite. Attila the Hun demanded a ton of pepper as a ransom for the city of Rome. It was often used for rentals and in payments of taxes. You still have some peppercorn rents in England." He pointed to some perennial climbing vines, the berries of which grew in clusters like tiny grapes. Some of them were just beginning to turn red and were therefore ready for plucking. "That's pepper," he told her.

"What happens to the berries after they're picked?"

"They're dried until they turn black and wrinkled. White pepper is got by macerating them after they've been well soaked in water." He squashed a berry for her to smell, and, sure enough, it did smell strongly of the pepper she was accustomed to seeing on the table.

"I'd love to see some cinnamon!" she exclaimed. "It was the cinnamon that brought you Dutch here, wasn't it?"

Hendrik made a wry face. "Those were times better forgotten. We didn't behave well. We were a little better than the Portuguese, who were here before us, because we were less cruel than they, but we were just as greedy, taking much more than we wanted to give back to the island. No European saw anything wrong in exploiting other peoples in those days!"

"Some don't now!" Michal softened the comment with a saucy smile, but she still meant him to know that she was talking about the way he was exploiting her.

"It's for your own good," Hendrik objected.

"It always was!" Michal reminded him.

"Not always," he said, almost sadly. "We'll have a good life together, caring for one another. In those days nobody cared. Cinnamon flourished wild in ancient Lanka, and we made our fortune by enslaving the peelers and forcing them to bring back more and more of the precious bark to the coast in tribute from the Sinhalese kings. We sentenced to death anyone caught giving away or selling a single stick. It was an unimaginative move; because of it, we soon lost the island to you British, first to your East India Company. Then, when they'd proved themselves to be about as indifferent to the welfare of the local inhabitants as we had been, the British government took over and began to develop the whole island, instead of only the coastal strip."

"Yet the van der Aas are still here," Michal murmured.

"Still selling cinnamon. I told you, we're a stubborn people and hang onto that which we have."

"You should have hung onto Marika!"

"Forget Marika!" he advised her.

But she shook her head. "Tante Willy looks just like her. You would be happier with someone like her. She might even understand what you're about in wanting a wife you've never met, because you'll never explain it to me!"

He looked amused. "It's an old family custom. My mother was Tante Willy's sister. They came out here together to marry the van der Aa brothers. Their marriages worked out—more or less."

"Tante Willy doesn't look like a happy woman to me!" Michal observed.

His amusement was gone. "No. She never really settled here in Sri Lanka, and when she broke her back it was the last straw. My mother was different. She was a warmer, more loving person altogether. I'd hoped Marika would be like her."

"But you didn't care enough to find out?"

His jaw tightened angrily. "Tante Willy made the arrangements. Marika was her choice. She would have done well enough, I dare say."

"You don't know Marika!" Michal retorted. "The world has taken a turn or two since Tante Willy and your mother were sold into bondage to the van der

Aa brothers. Women make their own decisions in Europe these days, or hadn't you heard?"

His amusement returned. "Here, we take what we're sent and are thankful. You won't make me change my mind about to-morrow now, my Michal!"

She sighed. "It wasn't really a promise at all—and you know it!"

His eyes filled with light. "I shall hold you to it—all the way!"

"But why?" she pleaded with him to tell her. "There must be other suitable women in the world!"

He turned away, shrugging. "Not for me," he said abruptly. "What else d'you want to see while we're here?"

She said the first thing that came into her head. "Vanilla!" Now, why vanilla? she wondered. She didn't even greatly care for the taste of the few pods which had come her way.

His attention was caught, however, his eyes narrowing as he looked at her. "Was that a deliberate choice, or just chance that you should choose the one crop which is too far away for us to look at now?"

She swallowed. "Chance," she admitted.

But he was still suspicious. She could tell by the calculating way he considered her, stroking at his chin with his long, strong fingers. She wished suddenly, urgently, that they were stroking her, and the colour flared into her cheeks, weakening her limbs so drastically that she longed to sit down.

"The vanillery is too far away to go there now. It's a lonely spot—the ideal place to be alone, one might say," he told her dryly.

"Then, by all means, let's give it a miss," Michal forced herself to say with an indifference she was far from feeling. She had to be mad to want to be *alone* with Hendrik, more alone than they were now!

"We'll go there some other time," he said. "Vanilla grows on vines, too, incidentally. But there are many other things for you to see now, like cardamom, cloves, nutmeg, coriander, and turmeric. Mace comes from nutmeg, and so we grow that, too. Would you like to see some of those?"

She made some sound of agreement, cautiously testing out her reactions to his touch on her arm. She was relieved to discover that things were back to normal, and apart from a slight tingling from the contact, she could walk and talk like an ordinary human being again.

Michal very much enjoyed the tour from one aromatic plant to the next. Hendrik took the trouble to explain exactly what she was looking at and how each spice was obtained in its season: the cardamom seeds nestling in their own capsules; the cloves, which were the undilated flower buds of an evergreen tree; nutmeg, which came from the pulpy fruits of another evergreen tree that could grow up to fifty or sixty feet in height; ginger, the tuber of a reed-like plant; coriander, used in bulk in curries; and turmeric, which came from tiny yellow tubers and was ground into a fine powder or paste.

"We try to keep a specimen of each plant here in the garden," Hendrik explained. "Lots of people like to come and look at them all growing together. We make a good thing out of selling sachets of the spices to tourists and others. It's only a sideline to our real business, but a profitable one."

Michal could imagine that it would be. Her own eye had been caught by the collections of spices that were laid out on tables in the sheds, and she had thought how pretty each collection was in its own right. They looked unusual and interesting—and their combined smell was overpowering! She hated to think what they would have cost if she had tried to buy them in England, but here they were very reasonably priced and done up in such generous quantities that most of them would have lasted the ordinary person a lifetime.

"What happens to them when they leave here?" she asked.

"The major spice markets are in London. One day, when we visit your country, I'll take you to see them. There are huge warehouses beside the Thames where they store the imported spices and export them again."

"Is that where yours go?"

He responded with a smug smile. "I've always got on well with the English," he teased her. "That's why I have no qualms about marrying one of them."

"You didn't send to England for a bride!" she reminded him tartly. "Not that anyone would have come if you had!"

"*You* came!"

"I was tricked into it by Marika—"

He actually had the audacity to laugh at her. "A businessman doesn't enquire how the sample gets on his desk. He backs his judgement on what he sees and, if he's a good businessman, makes his fortune by being right. I have never yet made a serious mistake."

"There's always a first time!" Michal snapped.

"Why don't you, too, settle for what you can get?" Hendrik taunted. He stood in front of her, blocking her path, his thumbs resting on the waistband of his cream-coloured trousers.

"Because marriage isn't a *business!* Just because *you* don't have a romantic bone in your body—like all the Dutch!—it doesn't mean we all value everything in terms of pounds, shillings, and pence!"

He was still laughing. "What d'you know about Dutch *men,* little one, that you think you know all about us?"

She blinked. "I know Marika!"

He lowered his voice to an intimate growl. "Have you ever known a Dutch man? Or any man?"

Michal recovered herself with difficulty. "Englishmen are far more romantic!" she insisted.

"Tell me that to-morrow!" Hendrik dared her, completely sure of himself.

"I know all I need to know about romance now," she maintained stubbornly, "and you don't appear in the picture at all."

His eyes were two green lakes in which it would be the easiest thing in the world to drown. Michal swallowed, wondering if she dared to swing away from him, leaving him standing where he stood. What could he do to her, after all? She might even get as far as the car and drive off and leave him there. She could imagine his fury with both himself and with her if she did anything of the kind.

His hand shot out and grasped hers. "I shouldn't!" he warned.

"Wouldn't do what?" she challenged him.

"Run. You may despise money, but you need it to get off the island, my dear. You need it for quite a lot of other things, too."

"For what?" she demanded crossly.

His voice was as smooth as silk. "Not for this, but for almost everything else." His lips touched hers, igniting a fuse of desire that shot through her bloodstream, bearing the message to every part of her.

She shivered, her fright clearly visible in her hazel eyes. "Please don't," she whispered.

"Don't what?"

He was whispering, too, his mouth close against hers. He put a hand on the nape of her neck and guided her head into a better angle for his kiss.

"That!" Michal gasped.

He rubbed his beard-roughened cheek against the softness of hers. "How long will you go on disapproving of me?" he asked her quietly. "Or is it yourself you disapprove of more?"

"I haven't done anything!" she disclaimed.

She could feel the laughter in his chest hard against her breasts, and the quick breath he took to still it, his arms tightening about her. She lifted her mouth to his, unable to resist the temptation of tasting his kiss again. Her lips parted under the crushing demand of his, but she made no attempt to escape the compelling mastery of his embrace.

His hands flattened behind her shoulder blades, holding her closer still. Then one hand explored each individual bone in her spine and on, down to her hips, reminding her how vulnerable she was to the hard masculinity of his body.

An instant later she was free, with only her hands held tightly in his in case she should fall.

"Do you still want to run?"

His voice came to her from a great distance. She could hardly hear it at all for the buzzing in her head and the pounding of her heart against her ribs.

"What did you say?"

Her ears cleared by magic and she was laughing up at him. Why should she run away? She liked Sri Lanka, she was almost sure she was falling in love with Hendrik, and there were enough precious gems to keep her professionally occupied for the rest of her life. She wanted nothing more at that moment, and she doubted if she ever would again.

The tense look on his face drained slowly away and a smile touched the corners of his lips. "You heard!" His smile grew broader. "I do believe you're coming round to my way of thinking!" Hendrik accused her.

Michal put her head to one side, astonished by this stranger who had come to life again inside her, this alter ego that had no patience with her fears for the future. This other self was eager and willing to become Mrs. van der Aa in the morning; moreover, she was only sorry there had to be any delay at all.

"You may have more to lose than I have," Michal heard this stranger say in light, mocking tones. "I know more about you than you do about me."

He traced her lips with his forefinger. "Do you?"

She nodded vigorously. "Marry me, and you have one or two shocks in store!"

"Really? Like what?"

She bit his finger lightly. "Michal had Joost—and we were friends. We shared more than our school days—"

"Not much more!"

The flat certainty of the words made the stranger inside her vanish, leaving her every bit as uncertain as she had been before.

"You can't *know* anything about me!" she repeated, more to convince herself than him.

"I know enough, Michal Brent." He ran his fingers through her hair as if he were dealing with a tiresome child. "And one of the things I know about you is that you'll come as a virgin to my bed!"

She was more shocked then she had thought possible that he could say such a thing out loud. She felt hot all over and she primped up her lips, wondering if her parents would have approved of him, after all. Then, quite suddenly, she laughed out loud.

"You can't *know* that!" she said with a sudden lightening of her spirits.

His glance was superior and very, very knowing. "I'd bet my bottom dollar on it!" he said. And the kiss he gave her was so swift and fleeting that she put a hand up to her mouth to convince herself that she hadn't imagined it.

Chapter Seven

Michal turned over with a mumbled protest as Belle tried to wake her up. It seemed to her she had only been asleep for five minutes, and this was the day she had been half-hoping would never dawn. This was the day of the full moon and her wedding day.

Belle put a cup of tea down on the table beside the bed and crossed the room to open the screens that kept the insects out at night. When she saw the chaos that greeted the sudden rush of light, she clicked her tongue in disapproval.

"Michal, what have you been doing? This is a bedroom for sleeping in, not a place to work the night hours away! Mr. Hendrik will have something to say about this!"

"I couldn't sleep," Michal excused herself, yawning. "And I don't see that it's any of Hendrik's business."

"He'll soon make it his business! What are all these instruments?" Her dark eyes widened dramatically as she took in something else. "What have you been boiling up in that?"

"Silver."

"In your *bedroom?*"

"I haven't anywhere else to work. It's all Hendrik's fault! He suggested I should make my own wedding ring, providing I got it finished by this morning. When I couldn't sleep, I thought I'd have a go at it. I made one for him, too, while I was about it. They're on the table over there."

Belle was impressed. Her tiny form flitted across the room to have a look, picking up the two rings and studying them from every angle.

"All these instruments are necessary to make these?" she cooed. "How clever you are, Michal! They're beautiful! Oh, look, you've written his name inside *both* rings! I can read van der Aa because it's my name, too." She giggled unexpectedly. "Sometimes it's my name, when I remember the funny ways Europeans have. I have my own name, too, of course."

"I'd like to be Michal Brent until I die," Michal said tragically.

But Belle only laughed. "That's why you made these rings, I suppose? What is this pattern on the outside?"

Michal yawned again, abandoning all further thoughts of sleep. "The roses of England and the tulips of Holland. There's a magnifying glass round somewhere. You can see them better through that.''

Belle did as she was told. There was a pregnant silence, and then she whispered, ''They're beautiful, Michal. The detail is perfect—''

Michal stuck out her tongue at Belle. ''Of course! No matter what the job is, I always do the best work I possibly can. It's a matter of pride!''

Belle nodded enthusiastically. ''Mr. Hendrik will be very proud!''

''Will he?'' Michal couldn't believe that. ''He'd probably prefer a plain gold band like a curtain ring, exactly the same as millions of others. Most people do!''

''Not Mr. Hendrik! Hans didn't like the unusual, but Mr. Hendrik isn't like his cousin. He chose *you*, Michal!''

Michal leaned back against the pillows with a wry smile. ''Lucky old me! Not that he did choose me—he had me wished on him as a temporary stopgap by Marika.''

Belle giggled. ''Mr. Hendrik decides things for himself. You'll find out! Tante Willy is always trying to manipulate him, as she did Hans, but Mr. Hendrik goes his own way. He's a stubborn man, that one!''

''It's such fun,'' said Michal, ''being married out of hand to a man because he can't bear to be the loser in anything!''

Belle looked uncertain. ''You're joking because you don't really want to go away. You forget that Mr. Hendrik may be a Dutchman, but his home is here, amongst us. He looks on people differently from those natives of Tante Willy's village. If people are good and kind, we forget the way they look."

"Thanks!" said Michal.

Belle laughed. "You see! You want him to notice that your hair is the colour of dying leaves and that you have soft skin, not the loneliness inside you and the pleasure you take in being one of a family like ours."

Michal was shaken by her perception. "Nevertheless," she objected, "men do look at women all the time—and not because they want to know what they're like inside!"

Belle picked up the wedding rings again, convulsed with laughter at some joke of her own.

"Poor Michal! How long will you hide your love for him?"

"I don't even like him!"

Belle's even teeth flashed against the deep brown of her skin. "When he sees how carefully you've made these rings, he'll know," she warned her, her eyes dancing with pleasure at the thought. Then, when Michal opened her mouth to contradict her, Belle added, *"Of course* he'll know."

"It's only a physical attraction. You can't build much of a marriage on that!"

Belle's smile faded. "You say that because you've never loved a man, but I can tell you, love like that can be stronger than death. It was between Hans and me."

Michal stayed in her bed for a long time after Belle had gone to start breakfast in the kitchen. She felt as though all her innards had collapsed, leaving her as vulnerable as a tortoise wrenched out of its shell.

She knew she was right! No two people should consider marriage if their only meeting place was a physical one, and there were only a few hours left for her to escape such a fate. If Marika hadn't answered her telegram, perhaps Tante Willy would help her.

She got out of bed with a grimace, determined to have a brisk shower and to lessen her feelings of self-pity. What she needed was a clear head and strong nerves, not to let Hendrik discover she was a mass of quivering jelly inside because there was no real love lost between them! It was even more ridiculous to suppose she could catch the mocking echoes of her other self's laughter. There was love, a great reservoir of love nobody in her life had ever wanted to know about, and which she had always dammed up inside her, pretending it wasn't there at all. Now the barriers were already under stress, and she was appalled to think of what might happen if Hendrik should breach them. She could only think he would share her parents' distaste for anything that smacked of the emotional. A cool affection was as much as they had ever wanted from each other, and they had asked for even less than that from her.

Saman was in the kitchen when Michal put in her appearance, her hair still damp from her shower.

"Hullo," she said. "Do you have a holiday, too?"

The boy smiled back at her. "Two holidays. We have a holiday every full moon, and to-day I have a holiday because you and Hendrik are getting married."

"What's special about the full moon?" Michal asked.

His face lit with enthusiasm. "The lord Buddha

was born at the full moon in May; he died then, too; but, best of all, that was the time when he was enlightened."

"Sitting under his tree?" Michal put in, embarrassed by the boy's eagerness.

"A bo tree," Saman agreed.

Michal gave in to the intensity of his conviction. "If I go to the temple with your mother, what do I have to do?"

Saman was delighted to tell Michal. "Buddha isn't God," he reminded her. "He's respected, as are all enlightened men. One offers flowers. If one has none, there are plenty on the temple grounds for you to pick. Then you say, 'I reverence Buddha with these flowers so that the merit may help me towards liberation. As these flowers dry up and turn to dust, so will my body one day turn to dust.'" He tried to hide his curiosity, but he wasn't very successful. "Why d'you want to go with my mother to-day? The temple will be very crowded for the holiday."

Michal shrugged. "It was just an idea. I have nothing else to do." Nothing she wanted to do, she added to herself. What she ought to do was get in touch with Marika.

"It's hard to wait," Saman agreed solemnly. "Women are always waiting."

Michal grinned. "Children, too."

"Yes, children too," he sighed.

"What are you waiting for?" Michal prompted him, hoping to get to know him better.

A smile flashed across his face. "Breakfast!" Then he shook his head, sobering instantly. "I wait and wait until I'm old enough to go to the monastery. At least you'll marry to-day. The waiting for you is almost over."

"Only I don't want to get married," Michal was astonished to hear herself confiding. "I don't know Hendrik, and I don't think I want to!"

Saman's eyes twinkled. "In your chart it says you've both met many times before!"

"I don't believe in such things! I believe we live only once!"

"Do you? Yet you recognised him at once as an old friend."

"Or an old enemy!" she retorted.

The boy's smile was very like his mother's, with the same perfect rows of teeth. "Christians are told to love their enemies! You'll have to learn to practise what you preach!"

Michal laughed easily with him, finding comfort in something that, in an English boy, she would have condemned as unbecomingly precocious and all too easy to dismiss as nonsense.

If Belle was surprised to have a companion on her visit to the temple, she gave no sign of it. She was wearing a white sarong and a well-worn white bodice that left her midriff bare. White, she explained to Michal, was the colour of mourning, and she always wore it on holidays. It was on those days that she allowed herself to think of Hans and the problems his death had brought her. "I wish him 'long life' in my heart," she ended sadly. "He loved life and will surely be born again."

Michal had put on a button-through cotton frock for the occasion. She still hadn't the faintest idea what she was going to wear to her wedding—if she hadn't devised some ruse to escape what everybody else seemed to think was her natural fate. If white was the colour of mourning in Sri Lanka, she'd do better to choose a dark colour. She had a dress of scarlet silk that lit the flames of her hair, and she rather thought she'd wear that.

The women of the neighbouring villages had come from all over to visit the temple that day. They had flowers and plates of fruit in their hands as they stood in the courtyard and gossiped under the hot sun, waiting for the saffron-robed monks to come and organise them into some kind of procession in honour of the lord Buddha. When they saw Michal they flocked about her, and when they saw the flowers she had picked to bring with her, they were full of smiles and sly looks.

"They know why you've come," Belle whispered to her. "If we go inside now, they'll wait till we come out again before they make their own offerings. They understand that you feel shy at first."

Michal slipped her shoes off, placing them neatly side by side at the entrance. She thought the Hindu gods who guarded the portals of the temple to be hideous, but she also recognised the symbolism they portrayed even whilst she didn't wholly understand it. The gods had so many faces between them, and arms growing out of their torsos, all of them with long, supple fingers that were plainly double-jointed.

Once past these guardians of the doors, her first impression was one of brash, vivid colours: oranges, greens, yellows, and scarlets—all trying to catch and hold the eye. Belle explained that the four major statues in the centre of the shrine represented the last four Buddhas who had achieved enlightenment. The fifth statue, smaller and relatively insignificant, stood for the next Buddha, the next member of the human race who would liberate himself through his own efforts from the endless cycle of life and death, and the suffering that was involved in both.

Crowding round these central figures were many others, grouped together in scenes representing the various events in the life of the last Buddha: his royal birth; his marriage; his leaving home to become an itinerant monk; his eventual enlightenment; the first sermon; and finally his death, with him lying on his side, one foot retracted a little from the other in the conventional pose of death. Buddha asleep was always shown with his two feet level with one another.

Michal left her flowers before the kindliest looking of all the Buddhas. Cause and effect, she told herself, was what all these people believed in. Perhaps the merit she had gained by her visit would cast a glow over the ordeal before her. If it meant anything, surely her offering of the prettiest flowers she had been able to find in Hendrik's garden should have the effect of giving joy to someone, and why not herself? She touched the petals of the star-like jasmine, the sweet-smelling frangipani, and put her hands up in front of her face in an imitation of Belle. She didn't think of death at all, as Saman had instructed her she should; she was thinking, instead, of Hendrik and how different everything would be if he had chosen her as the wife of his heart, and not just as the only handy, unattached female round.

More and more people came to leave their garlands of flowers and plates of fruit. The food was eventually eaten by the monks, or fed to the patiently waiting birds that kept a respectful distance until they were called to the feast they were quite sure was coming. Mostly, Michal noticed, they were crows, which, though a not particularly gregarious bird in England, flocked happily together in Sri Lanka, cawing loudly to one another to come down and partake of the festive meal.

Monkeys, too, dodged expectantly between human feet, chasing their own tails and teasing the dogs, and holding out their tiny hands hopefully for pieces of coconut, bananas, and, best of all, freshly cooked corn on the cob.

"It will soon be the day of Belle's almsgiving," one of the women who could speak a little English said to Michal. "Will you be helping her? She is glad to have you in the house."

Michal was both pleased and startled to find Belle had spoken well of her. "What happens at an almsgiving?" she asked.

The woman smiled and shook her head. "Belle will tell you that when the time comes."

The queue of worshippers moved on and, at last, Belle was ready to go.

"What is an almsgiving?" Michal asked her on the way home.

Belle slanted a smile. "One gives alms—what else?" She hurried her steps, plainly embarrassed that it should have been suggested to Michal that she might be required to help on the great day. "One gives to the monks," she went on to explain. "Usually one chooses the anniversary day of a parent's death, but in my case it will be Hans' day. You'll know all about it when it happens."

Tante Willy had already been carried out onto the verandah when they got home. Michal greeted her eagerly.

"Have you heard from Marika?" Michal pressed her.

"Nothing."

Michal's shoulders sagged. "What am I to do? Tante Willy, you must help me!"

"Why should I?"

"You don't want me here. You'd be delighted if I went back to England and Hendrik married someone from your old village."

"True," the Dutch woman responded. "I was looking forward to having someone of my own here. When I came out here, I had my sister for company. She was the more fortunate of the two of us— always! I wanted to marry the older brother because, by rights, everything should have belonged to him. We all know that younger brothers have to make their own way in the world and are often not very good at it! But with the van der Aas, it was the younger brother who had all the backbone. They had a very happy marriage and a fine son to show for it!"

"You had Hans," Michal said gently.

Tante Willy snorted her contempt. "He was like his son! The only normal thing he ever did was to marry Belle. She's so pretty it was impossible for even that one to overlook her!"

Michal sat down on the vacant chair beside the older woman. "What was your husband like?" If she asked that, she thought, she could ask about Hendrik's parents later. She was surprised how badly she wanted to know about them.

Tante Willy glanced across at her with her customary asperity. "I didn't miss him much. I missed my sister far more. I fought with her constantly, but she's the one I really miss now. I'm lonely without her."

"Hence, your hopes of Marika? You wouldn't have nearly as much in common with her as you think."

"What have I in common with you?"

"Nothing," Michal admitted. "So why don't you help me to go back to England?"

"Because I haven't any money of my own," Tante Willy snapped.

"No money?" Michal simply didn't believe her. "You must have money of your own! What about the money your husband left you?"

"He'd long ago sold out to his younger brother. No, no, my dear, Hendrik owns everything that bears the name van der Aa. My family lives on his charity, all three of us. We have nothing of our own!"

Michal digested this in silence. "It looks as though we're stuck with each other," Michal said at last, "unless Marika answers my telegram in the nick of time."

"She won't," Tante Willy decided wearily. "She's

another one to cut off her nose to spite her face —just as I was at her age! When she finally wakes up to what's happened, though, she's going to hate you for being Hendrik's wife."

"And will you hate me, too?" Michal asked sadly.

"Marika is my kinswoman," Tante Willy answered stubbornly. "You're a foreigner, and a fool. I wouldn't mind so much if you appreciated your luck in catching Hendrik on the rebound, but all you do is mope and send Marika silly messages you know she won't bother to answer. Take what Hendrik offers you and be thankful! He'll take what he wants from you. Why don't you do the same to him?"

"Marika is my friend—" Michal began hopelessly.

"More fool you!"

Tante Willy's neighing laugh brought Michal close to losing her temper. She stood up, nearly knocking her chair over as she did so.

"It isn't *things* I want in a marriage!" she exclaimed bitterly. "I want my husband to be in love with me!"

"And how long would that last?" was the older woman's cynical reply. "A year or two? A sound marriage has always been based on property and mutual advantage, my dear. Why should yours be any different?"

It was a philosophy that Michal couldn't, and wouldn't, subscribe to. At least her own parents' gentle affection for each other had been better than that, though their marriage had left much to be desired, in her opinion. She herself wanted to know the heights of love, and if that meant knowing the depths, as well, it would be worth it. If Hendrik were to whisper one word of love to her—

Her eyes met Tante Willy's derisive glance and she walked away from her, striving to regain control over her own volatile emotions. It was unfortunate that Hendrik should choose that moment to join them. Michal walked straight into his solid, hard body, not seeing him at all, and it was only his quick reactions in fielding her that prevented her from falling over his feet. Her pulse quickened as she freed herself from the strong grasp of his hands. She longed to fling herself into his embrace and wondered bleakly what he would do if she were to give in to such a wanton impulse.

"You look tired, *meisje*," Hendrik commented. "Belle tells me you were up working all night. Aren't you going to show me the results of your labours?"

Michal tossed her hair back out of her face. "I'm sure Belle will show you—if you ask her nicely, or even if you don't!"

Silently, he opened his hand to reveal the two rings in his palm. "Don't blame Belle," he warned her. "She thought they might get lost unless they were put in a place of safety."

"I don't blame Belle for anything!" Michal assured him quickly. She sought for some way of getting rid of him whilst a small piece of her dignity was still intact. "Go away! It's very bad luck for us to meet to-day of all days!"

His fingers took possession of her chin, forcing her head back so that she had no chance of avoiding the knowing look in his eyes. "I'm glad to find you taking your wedding day so seriously," he said teasingly.

Her eyes swam with tears. "Why don't you let me go?" she demanded.

"I need a wife!"

"*Any* wife?" she shot at him.

He touched his lips to hers and felt the inevitable jolt of response as she tried to avoid his kiss, failed, and then sobbed out his name in disbelief at the treachery of her own flesh.

"You need a husband, too," he pointed out, drawing her along the corridor towards her bedroom. His green eyes mocked her. "I like this English word 'husband.' A man should husband his wife, sharing what he has with her. Is that such a bad thing?"

"I don't want any of your possessions! I'd rather fend for myself than have to rely on some man to do it for me!"

"I see. You think in marriage all things must be equal? Is that why you made two wedding rings?"

She shrugged her shoulders. "Some men like to wear a ring," she said indifferently. "It doesn't mean anything."

She closed her eyes to shut out the green flash of triumph in his eyes. Why had she been such a fool as to write his name on both rings? What utter folly! She opened her eyes again. Any hope she might have had that he had made only a cursory examination of the rings died even as she did so. Belle had been talking! An excited, proud Belle, who had never seen anything like the two wedding rings before, had pointed out every feature to him, holding the magnifying glass in the way that Michal had herself taught her, so that Hendrik could read the neatly engraved name of van der Aa running round the inside of them both.

"It doesn't mean a thing!" she reiterated. "It was too hot to sleep, that's all, and I wanted to make sure I hadn't lost my touch. You can force me to marry you to-day, but as soon as I've gathered enough money together for the flight home, you won't be able to keep me here!"

His expression was surprisingly gentle. "When the time comes, you may not want to go. The tulips and roses on the rings go well together." He glanced down at them. "Was it your desire for independence that made you put the tulips on the outside, guarding the roses of England, on both rings?"

"They're meant to be a pair!"

His smile made her heart knock violently against her ribs. "The wearers are meant to be a pair, too!"

"A pretty ill-assorted pair!"

He put his head to one side, watching the troubled movement of her mouth. "Not bad," he said. Very slowly he licked his lips, his eyes never leaving her face. It was the most sensuous gesture Michal had ever seen. Her whole body burned as she imagined it was her lips he had touched with his tongue, and she was hard put not to moisten them in his stead. "At least we have one thing in common," he remarked.

Michal blinked, hoping to break the spell. "Marika may have changed her mind! I'm sure she meant it as a joke when she sent me here on my own. What will you do if she arrives to-morrow—or the next day?"

"She'll be welcome—as a friend of *yours*. She may amuse Tante Willy for a while if you want her to stay and give you moral support, as you were going to do for her."

Michal sighed. "She won't like it!" she blurted out. "I think we ought to wait and see if she comes, after all. She may even want to marry you!"

Hendrik put the two rings carefully away in his pocket. "Too bad, Michal, my golden rose! It'll be too late, either way. I have your promise as surely as I have our wedding bands!"

And her heart, too, only he didn't know it, which was more than Marika would have brought to her wedding. Marika would have taken his kisses and his worldly goods, but what would she have given him in return? It wasn't much comfort, however, to know that Hendrik didn't care either way. Any woman would do for him! So why couldn't he have found some other woman besides the one who had been fool enough to fall in love with him? Any other woman but the unfortunate Miss Michal Brent.

Chapter Eight

It wasn't the way Michal had always fondly imagined she would be transported to her wedding. She had always thought to meet her husband at the altar, for them to be very much in love with each other, and for her to have all her friends about her. The contrast with this lonely trip to Galle, with Hendrik driving the car, was too poignant for words. Worse still, it had begun badly, with Michal making one last attempt to talk Hendrik out of marrying her.

"I'm not going to Galle with you," she had told him. "I'm not going to marry you. You can't make me go through with this stupid ceremony!"

He had looked at her, his eyes cold. "No? How are you going to live if you don't marry me?"

"I'll get myself deported as an undesirable!"

"But"—and his voice had pierced her like splinters of ice—"I wouldn't let that happen to you, Michal Brent. I don't want my wife to have any such disaster written into her passport."

"I wouldn't be your wife if I were back home in England!" she had retorted.

"I shouldn't rely on it," he had advised her. "Marry me you will!"

She had thrown back her head. "Will I? We'll see!" She had thrown down the gauntlet.

He had lifted her into his arms in a way he had no right to do. She was too heavy for any man to do such a thing to her! And he had laughed out loud, apparently enjoying the exercise.

"Don't tempt me, Michal," he had said, and he had meant it. "I think you'll prefer to have one of your exquisite rings on your finger before I give in to our mutual need to make love."

"But it isn't going to be that sort of marriage!" she had exclaimed, kicking her feet in the air in the hopes of making contact with his shins.

His only response had been to hold her tighter still, until her breasts had ached with the pressure of the hard wall of his chest—and with something else that she had belatedly recognised as a burgeoning panic of excitement at finding herself so close to him.

A moment later he had placed her on the front seat of his car, stooping over to deliver a hard kiss on her mouth, before he closed the door on her.

They had gone through several of the fishing villages on the way to Galle before she had recovered sufficiently to make sense of the scenery they were passing through. She awoke from her dream of what-might-have-been to notice several fishermen, their sleek, black bodies dressed only in the skimpiest of G-strings, pulling in their nets, which were bulging with fish. Their mates were already planting white and yellow flags on the beach, proclaiming the wealth of their catch to the whole village.

"They'll all eat well tonight," Hendrik remarked, frowning at her pale features.

"I thought it was a holiday," Michal demurred.

"Some people can't afford to take a holiday if they work with the sea or the land. The fish are running, so they go to work."

Michal wished Belle and Saman had travelled in the same car with them. It would have lightened the atmosphere, and she would have been sure of their company on the way home. She didn't want to be alone with Hendrik. Indeed, she felt all hot and bothered at the thought of it. She wasn't going to be able to keep him at arm's length forever.

The kilns that burned the coral for the making of cement had mostly shut down for the day, but the people were still crowding the road, walking in the hot sun. There were numerous piles of the orange king coconuts waiting to be sold to a passing motorist at every corner. Michal considered asking for one to quench her thirst, but one look at Hendrik's determined profile changed her mind.

In another village they had plaited the still-green palm leaves into a triumphal arch and had decorated the street with plaited ties of the same leaves, looking like simple corn-dollies, hanging on strings that stretched from one telephone pole to another.

"Is that in honour of the holiday?" Michal made herself speak, keeping her voice as normal as possible.

"Someone's died in the village," Hendrik answered. "The funeral pyre will be a little way outside the village. It will be decorated, too."

"It must be someone very important," Michal commented.

"Not necessarily. Most people insure with the cooperatives for their funeral expenses. They like to think they'll have a good send-off."

"I suppose we all do," Michal agreed.

"She was younger than you are," Hendrik said abruptly. "No one knows why she died."

Michal was shocked by his fatalism. "Wasn't there an inquest? Or at least a death certificate?"

"We're a long way from Colombo here. This isn't Europe, where everyone has a doctor close at hand." His hands tightened on the steering wheel. "Here, we do the best we can and accept what we can't afford to do—yet! One day, girls like her will live as long as their Western counterparts—please, God."

She was touched by his concern. Perhaps he wasn't as impregnable as she had imagined, but would she ever be able to storm the fortress behind which he hid his heart?

"Did you know her?" Michal asked him.

"Belle did. Belle knows everyone along this road. She came from one of the villages between here and Galle, and she's always lived hereabouts. She and Hans were going to go and live in Holland, but he died before they could get away. She'll never move far from Saman now, whatever he chooses to do, and so it looks as though she's here for life."

"How did Hans die?"

"He took the family for a helicopter ride. He, my parents, and his father were killed. Tante Willy broke her neck and has been paralysed ever since. It was a black day for all of us." His voice hardened. No wonder, Michal thought, that Hendrik often seemed dogmatic and cold. He had lost a great deal in his life at an early age. The responsibilities had been crushing. There had been little time for the gentler emotions, the more subtle shadings.

Galle was a bigger town than Michal had realised from their visit there the day before. It seemed to be filled with ox-drawn taxis, small converted carts that were bulging with passengers and their possessions. Those vehicles that weren't taxis were also ox-drawn, the patient beasts waiting endlessly in the sun for their owners to load and unload the typical carts, with their even more typical woven-matting sides.

Sometimes, Michal noticed with glee, an ox would cross its legs in the front, thus aiding the primitive braking system, which was no more than a piece of wood on wires that caught up behind the wheels and stopped the cart from running away downhill. The animals of Sri Lanka were not chattel, but partners in any task they undertook, a fact acknowledged by them and the human beings who owned them.

Going into the old Dutch fort was like going into another world. Here, the buildings could only have been Dutch. The church could have been uprooted stone by stone from any town or village in the

Netherlands. Inside, it had that same empty, well-swept look of all the Protestant churches of Northern Europe.

With a wave of relief, Michal saw that Belle and Saman were already there, waiting for them. Belle was wearing her very best sarong, covered by a sari of the same material that she had pinned to her shoulder with a brooch that shot daggers of fire into the air as she walked. She smiled warmly at Michal and placed an enormous bouquet of the same flowers she had herself chosen to take to the temple that morning in her arms.

"From your new family," she whispered, "to give happiness to the bride."

Michal felt the tears pressing at the back of her eyes. She longed to cry out, to beg Belle not to be too kind to her, lest she should break down altogether. What had happiness to do with this ceremony, which was as empty as the church it was taking place in?

Michal should have felt the pleasant contrast from the burning heat outside, but all she felt was so frozen inside that she could barely stop herself from shivering. Nor did she understand anything that anyone said to her. She imagined that most of the stolid, fair-haired burghers and their wives had spoken to her in English, but it could equally as well have been Dutch. She remembered laughing to herself because the burghers of Sri Lanka could have stepped out of the paintings of any of their ancestors, despite the mixture of blood their wives had brought to them over the generations.

The pastor she understood least of all, and so she

was completely unprepared for the moment when Hendrik put the smaller of the two wedding rings on her finger. His smile was very gentle, and her heart turned over within her at the sudden rush of warmth that passed through. Her own fingers were trembling as the pastor held out the second ring to her on the opened pages of the prayer book, and she stared at it blankly for a long moment before she recovered herself sufficiently to pick it up and place it in turn in Hendrik's outstretched hand.

Had she made it too small? She thought it wouldn't go on, but it slid easily into place at last as he put his own fingers over hers to help her press it home.

"You may kiss the bride," the pastor said in heavily accented English.

"I mean to—often!" Hendrik said in her ear.

She emerged from the embrace with her cheeks flushed and her hair tousled, and with something like a sensation of triumph in her heart. At least in public he hadn't failed her. He had made her look like the much-loved woman any bride was supposed to be. It wasn't true, of course—would never be true for her—but for an instant, the bells had rung and the flowers had given up their scent, and she had been totally happy to be in his arms.

"Well, Mrs. van der Aa, are you coming to the dance?"

"What dance?" Michal thought she had lost the capacity to be surprised by anything that day, but it seemed she was wrong.

He leant across the table towards her and the light

131

of the candles was reflected in the flames in his eyes.
"The *Bali-Thovil* dance—devil-dancing. They go on
until dawn, so we won't stay until the end, just long
enough to give you a taste of something which is
very much a part of my country."

Devil-dancing? Were they never to be alone? But
then, what reason did he have to want to be alone
with her? So far, he had filled in every moment of
the day with an audience of strangers. First, there
had been the wedding celebrations in the company
of his friends amongst the burghers; it had been a
dull, formal affair, made worse by the knowledge
that these stolid men and women were unlikely to
approve of her.

After that he had taken her to look at Galle's
harbour, the great international ships, and the fishing boats that smelt of fish, and he had told her why
the Dutch had built such a large fort on that
particular site in the first place. He had pointed out
the badge over the entrance gate and had brought
out from his pocket one of the old Dutch coins of the
island that bore the same device.

He hadn't kissed her in all that time. He hadn't so
much as touched her. Indeed, he had avoided even
looking at her, almost as if he wished she were
someone else and couldn't bear the disappointment
of being confronted with her features, instead. Was
that her imagination? She sighed, wishing for the
hundredth time that he was as much in love with her
as she was with him.

She pushed her helping of fish curry from one side
of her plate to the other. "Devil-dancing," she
repeated. "It must be very old."

"Older than Buddhism," he agreed. "Probably older than Hinduism. It once had a ritual significance that is mostly lost now, though it's sometimes still used to cure people of certain maladies, or to bring a private grief into the public domain. The community aspect is very important."

"Then why are we going?" She picked at her food some more, wondering why it never seemed to be disappearing from her plate.

He looked at her for a long moment, his impatience draining away what little confidence she had left. "It's my community," Hendrik said at last. "I belong here. We both belong here."

No! She did not! She never would belong to the island—no more than he belonged to her!

"I expect I'll enjoy it," Michal murmured languidly. "I've always liked music and the dance."

"Good. Have you had enough of that curry?"

She nodded her head. Her mouth felt stiff and she realised that, although she had a smile fixed on her face, it was no more than a facade, hiding her insecurity and the feeling she had that she was going to prove completely inadequate for the challenge of being married to Hendrik.

"Tante Willy thought we might have gone to Kandy," she confided.

"Is that what you wanted to do?"

She had an idea that Kandy was romantic and beautiful. She had seen pictures of a lake and of the famous Temple of the Sacred Tooth, where the tooth of Buddha rested on a golden lotus leaf, under seven crystal covers, behind three doors—one of silver, one of gold, and one of ivory.

133

"Ours isn't that kind of marriage."

His eyes narrowed. "What makes you say that?"

She was too weary not to be honest. "You've been hoping I'll turn into someone else all day."

There was a moment's silence, and the truth came to her like a bolt from the blue, and with it all her hopes collapsed into a pitiful little heap at her feet.

"Was *she* killed in the helicopter crash, too?"

He didn't pretend not to understand her, and, for that, she supposed, she ought to have been grateful. "Yes, she was," he said.

She licked her lips. "Were you going to take her to Kandy?"

"Probably."

"Then I suppose we're better off here." She tried to force another smile, but her mouth insisted on turning down at the corners. No wonder he didn't care who he married if he couldn't have the one woman he wanted. "I expect I'll enjoy the devil-dancing just as much!" she declared valiantly. But she turned her face away from him, all the same.

His ring flashed in the candlelight, catching her eye. "I'll take you to Kandy one day, but not to-day," Hendrik promised gently.

"Because you couldn't bear the comparison?"

Michal hadn't meant to say that, or anything like it. She should have made him think she cared as little as he did, not sounded like a heartsick teen-ager, crossed in love for the very first time.

"You come out rather well in any comparison," he said surprisingly. "It's just that Kandy is a place apart, a dream place, and the sooner we get on with our real life together, the better."

It was something that he liked her, even if the spark wasn't there. She wondered what the other girl had been like. She must have been beautiful, she thought, and with more than her share of sex appeal. She couldn't imagine Hendrik falling for an ordinary girl—someone like herself.

She pushed her plate away from her. "What time does the devil-dancing begin? It would be a shame to be late."

His mouth twisted into a wry smile. "It wasn't the grand romance of your imaginings. I'll tell you about it someday."

"I don't want to know!"

He pushed back his chair and stood up. "You're right. The past is dead and gone, and better not remembered by either of us. Shall we go?"

It was dark and mysterious outside, a tropical night filled with the noise of insects and other nocturnal creatures. To Michal, the anonymity of the night was welcome. In the darkness she could pretend they were an ordinary couple with a secure future in front of them. She grabbed at Hendrik's arm to steady herself and she was suddenly laughing up at him, a different girl from the one who had sat opposite him at dinner. After all, it was she, not the poor dead girl, who was Mrs. Hendrik van der Aa, and she might as well make the best of it. She was pleasantly conscious of the hard muscles of Hendrik's arm beneath her fingers.

Michal recognised the village they came to as the same one where they had had the catch of fish that afternoon. They made their way to a clearing under the coconut palms. The full moon cast an eerie silver light over the scene which not even the kerosene lamps could dispel. In the centre of the clearing, a bonfire had been lit, but it had not yet burst into flames. A dull plume of smoke rose up between the heavy crowns of the palms, blotting out the brightness of the stars.

Hendrik was very much at his ease. He arranged for chairs to be brought, explaining that Michal would find the ground hard and uncomfortable if they stayed for long.

"Would you like some tea?" he asked her.

"Is it possible?"

"Of course. We're a hospitable people. But you may not care for the taste much. It isn't the same as the tea you're used to."

Michal was handed a glassful of steaming liquid which she thought was quite the nastiest drink she had had in a long time. It was tea, all right, but very sweet, and with the pungent addition of ginger, a flavour she had never cared for, and still didn't now.

"Give it to me!" Hendrik bade her under the cover of the darkness. He swallowed it down at a single gulp and gave her back the empty glass. "You'll have to get used to it," he told her. "It's always made this way on the island, and you're sure to be offered it wherever you go."

She made a face. "If it were either just sweet or gingery, I might get to like it, but both—!"

Hendrik chuckled, more friendly than he had been all day. "Belle will spread the word that you don't like sweet things but the villagers wouldn't consider it tea if it didn't have ginger in it. They always drink it that way."

While he was speaking the performers burst into the centre of the clearing. They were wearing the most grotesque and horrific masks that Michal had ever seen. Snakes appeared out of their mouths, and enormous, globular eyes rolled with extraordinary realism. She uttered a startled cry and felt Hendrik's hand on hers.

"They're the demons," he murmured, "eighteen in all, the causes of the illnesses the dance is supposed to help."

Michal clutched his hand in relief. They were funny, as well as terrifying, as each demon made a few introductory movements in time to the music. Then each one had to be placated by one of the other dancers, who offered gifts in exchange for the devil's departure. The bargaining was plainly ribald and the villagers shouted with laughter, throwing in an occasional comment themselves to help the proceedings along.

"How do they learn what to do?" Michal whispered to Hendrik during a pause in the music.

"The art is preserved in certain families. The dancers begin young under the tutelage of an uncle, father, or some other relation. The whole tradition is family and caste-orientated. At first the youngsters learn both how to dance and how to play the drums; they choose which they'll make their own when they're a bit older. The art is dying, but it still lives on in the smaller villages where there is little else to entertain the people."

Michal watched fascinated. Some of it she could translate for herself. She recognised that the fire and the aromatic smoke created by various powders thrown into the flames were ritual cleansing agents, and she supposed the twirling torches, the running of the naked flame across their skin, and even the fire "eating" were all extensions of the same idea. One by one, the demons were banished from the circle, and only the drummers were left.

Then the women came into their own, dancing the dances they had always danced, to safeguard the harvest and to bring the life-enhancing forces closer to all the members of their family. They came and went amongst the audience, including them all in their gentle, sinuous movements until even Michal felt a part of the dance, lost in the central myth that had woven all women together since the beginning of time.

"It's time to go," Hendrik said.

"Not yet," Michal pleaded.

She didn't want to leave this magic circle. She wasn't ready to face the problems that she knew awaited her. She wanted to stay here forever, an intimate part of the music and the whirling lights. Even the masks no longer frightened her. They made her want to laugh, and she was enchanted by the satirical element that their wearers could introduce into the most realistic of their dances.

Hendrik's fingers linked about her wrist and he pulled her inexorably to her feet. He looked very handsome in the moonlight, his hair so fair as to be white, and the glow of the firelight accentuated the strong line of his jaw and the firm moulding of his lips.

"It's time to go home," he said.

She sat beside him in silence all the way back to his house. When he turned into the drive, the sweet-smelling scent of the flowering bushes came drifting towards them, enhancing the poignancy of the need within her, a need she refused to express in words or even to acknowledge at all.

The house was quiet. Michal's eyes went straight to Tante Willy's door, but the telltale strip of light wasn't there. Apparently she, like the rest of the household, was fast asleep.

Michal licked her lips, pausing at the end of the corridor.

"Good night, Hendrik."

He watched her open her bedroom door. "Is this the way you really want it?"

"Until you've forgotten about *her*."

He came close, putting his arms about her and parting her lips with his own. She turned her head, her eyes heavy with an emotion she had never felt before. Silently, he held out his hand to her and she closed her door.

"It'll make it so final," she protested, "and we don't love each other."

He kissed her lips again, his hands finding and undoing the fastenings of her dress. "All I know about you is that I want you!"

Michal's stranger self came to life with a violence that was shattering in its intensity. She knew only triumph as she pressed herself against the hardness of his body, hugging him closer to her and putting her lips to his.

"Please hold me tight, Hendrik," she whispered, and was shocked to feel his hands against her naked breasts.

"I mean to, *meisje*. Come to bed, my sweet, and we may find that Paradise is closer than we thought!"

Chapter Nine

The touch of his hands spread a warm glow through her body that built up into a wave of happiness that she couldn't deny. It was a golden, beautiful moment snatched out of time, brighter than the flames of the torches the dancers had flourished in the velvet darkness, brighter even than the rays of the sun.

"Oh, Hendrik, don't stop now!" she gasped.

"I couldn't if I wanted to," he said.

"Tears, Michal? What's the matter?"

"No, it's nothing," she admitted.

His exasperated expression made her want to laugh. "I'll never understand women as long as I live!" Hendrik declared.

Michal was close enough to him to see that he

needed a shave. He was so fair that the stubble of his beard wasn't as obvious as it would have been with most men. She wondered if she would ever feel sufficiently at home with him to tell him how she liked the way his skin rasped hers when he kissed her. She smiled slowly, noticing the way his long lashes curled at the tips and were darker there than they were at the roots.

"I didn't want to marry you," she said. "I may not like being married to you."

His look was masculine, amused, and complacent. "Think not?"

She turned her hot cheeks away from his gaze. "You might not like being married to me," she persevered in shaken tones.

"I think I can bear it."

He picked up her left hand and spread it against his, palm to palm, so that the two wedding rings were touching.

"But you didn't want to marry *me*. Any woman would have done."

"Not any woman," he denied abruptly. He got out of bed with the sinuous grace of a hardened athlete, pulling on his robe as he did so. "Come on, lazybones," he threw at her. "We've just time to have a swim before breakfast if you hurry."

The idea was attractive. She waited for him to turn his back and made a dash across the room to the bathroom. When she came out again, he had gone, and she was able to don her swimming suit in comfort, without being fazed by his watchful presence. It was a consideration she had not expected from him. It seemed he knew far better than she which was the moment for action and which was for retreat, but then he was experienced in ways she was not and probably never would be.

"Are you ready?" he called outside her door.

She went out to join him, pulling on her sand shoes as she went. "We should have gone swimming by moonlight last night," she said.

Hendrik's appreciative glance swept over her. "We had other things to do!"

Michal pushed past him into the garden, plucking a star of jasmine from the bush by the door and twiddling it between her fingers.

"We could have done both," she said slowly. Then, unforgivably, she added, "Did your fiancée like to swim?"

"No. She was afraid of ruining her hair in the water."

With that fatal feeling that she was about to make things worse when she only wanted to make them better, Michal rushed on. "What about your other women?"

"What other women?"

He had turned the tables neatly on her, and it was she who was now rigid with embarrassment.

"I thought—"

"Yes?"

"There must have been other women!" she exclaimed in desperation.

"What I fail to see," he said slowly, "is what they have to do with you."

The road to the beach seemed only half as far as it had the first time Michal had walked along it. She

143

had to stride out to keep pace with Hendrik, because even in this, he made no allowances for someone else's frailty, expecting her to keep up with him, just as he had demanded her response when he had been making love to her. He had his own way far too often, she thought, and from there it was a natural progression to wonder if his fiancée would have handled him better if she had lived. Would she have known how to soften the hard corners of his character? How lucky she had been to have had his love!

The sea was as smooth as a silken robe as she dived through the white-topped waves and allowed herself to be carried back to the beach by abandoning herself to the incoming tide.

Farther out was a boy in an outrigger canoe. The sight made a pretty shape against the sky. She watched it lazily until it finally disappeared from sight, vanishing behind a group of coconut palms that leaned together in a tangle of leafy crowns, right at the edge of a small finger of land that jutted out into the water.

She was sorry when Hendrik said it was time to go back to the house. In the sea she could be as young and foolish as she liked, and there was no one to notice. Back on dry land, she had to face the rest of the van der Aas as both a married woman and one of themselves. It was a responsibility she could have done without. She felt as shy and as stupid at the thought as she had ever felt in her life.

"Hungry?" Hendrik asked her.

"Greedy, more like, for Belle's cooking!"

He grinned. "I shan't object to a little extra plumpness here and there," he teased her.

She tried to reply in kind. "My father always said all men are Turks at heart. He objected to having a string bean for a daughter, but I've filled out a bit since those days."

"My word, you have!"

The Australianism made her laugh. She wondered how he came to speak English so extraordinarily well, much better than any of the other burghers she had met. Then she looked down at herself, pleased that there were no signs of any unnecessary bulges anywhere. She looked very well in a swimming suit, she thought.

"I'll race you back to the house!" she challenged him.

"You're on!"

She arrived at the kitchen door only slightly behind him and collapsed into the nearest chair, panting hard with her efforts to beat him.

Belle looked round at her from the wood-fired stove, smiling. "You ought to know better than to play silly games in this heat," she rebuked her gently. "Mr. Hendrik has longer legs than you."

"I know. I have to run beside him when he's walking. That's why I thought I'd make him run, too!"

Belle shook her head, clicking her tongue. "There's a letter for you, Michal. I put it on the table."

Michal reached out a hand and picked up the pale mauve envelope. She recognised the handwriting at once, and the colour drained out of her face as she crumpled the corners between reluctant fingers. The letter was from Marika.

145

Marika's writing was a legacy from a former age. It was very large and it flowed across the paper without any empty spaces, taking up as much room as possible.

Hendrik's eyebrows rose as he glanced at the distinctive purple ink that the Dutch girl always used.

"It's from Marika," Michal told him.

"Never mind. Holland is a long way away."

"The Netherlands," she corrected him. "Marika gets cross if you call it Holland."

"So you said before," he remembered. He jerked a finger towards the letter. "Aren't you going to open it and see what she has to say?"

She went on holding it, much as if it were a bomb that was about to explode in her face. It was addressed, she noticed, to Miss Michal Brent, and so Marika had probably written it before she received Michal's telegram—if she ever had.

"Shall I do it?" Hendrik offered.

Michal clutched it to her. "It's my letter! It's nothing to do with you!"

He leaned back, his eyes lazy as he studied her guilty face. "My dear Michal, you look as though you'd stolen something from her and are about to be found out!"

"Why should I care?" Michal retorted. "She sent me here in her place and told me to enjoy myself!"

"So she did," he drawled. "And are you?"

Michal couldn't bring herself to answer him. She pushed the letter from one hand to the other and back again. It was bound to be bad news.

"Get on with it!" Hendrik advised her.

Michal put her finger under the seal and tore open the envelope with a sigh. The letter was several pages long, but as there were little more than half a dozen words on each page, the message wasn't lengthy at all.

"She's not going to marry Joost," Michal announced in a flat, defeated voice. "They're not compatible."

"Too bad," said Hendrik.

"She's taking the next plane out here—to marry you."

"Oh?" Hendrik's tone was as bleak as hers. "What makes her think she'll be welcome?"

Michal stared at him. She wished she could tell him about the hollow feeling in the pit of her stomach. What little confidence she had in her new role as Hendrik's wife shattered. He hadn't married her as a person in her own right, no matter how hard she tried to pretend to herself he had.

"She'll be furious!" Michal said heatedly.

His green eyes glinted. "And are you 'furious' too?"

She gulped. *"I don't know!"* But she did know. Anger was the last thing on her mind at the moment. She was far too busy coping with the agony of fear and jealousy that had hit her the moment she had seen Marika's writing on the envelope. At least Hendrik's beloved fiancée was dead; Marika was very much alive, and Michal had known her long enough to know that, when it came to getting her own way, she was completely unscrupulous.

147

He reached out a hand, fingering a copper lock of her hair. "Marriage lasts longer than one night, my dear," he said dryly.

"Marika might not consider us properly married."

He pulled on her hair as a warning not to say anymore. "She should have thought of that before. She's your friend, and she'll be your responsibility while she's here. At least Tante Willy should enjoy her visit."

Michal sniffed. "I wish she weren't coming," she said. It was all very well for him to say that Marika was her responsibility. He didn't know Marika. When he did, he'd wish he'd waited. All the men Michal knew had always preferred Marika to herself!

"Then tell her so," he recommended.

Her eyes opened wide. "I can't do that! I'm here only because of her!"

His look was suddenly intimate, bringing a blush to her cheeks. "I like to think it's because of me that you're only forty miles from Paradise. If you could only believe it, *meisje,* you might find you're even closer than that!"

"Marika isn't interested in romantic notions like the fountains of Paradise," she retorted primly.

Hendrik took her wedding ring between two of his fingers, turning the silver band over and over. "That's why I married you."

"You married me because I was conveniently on hand and couldn't get away from you!"

A muscle twitched in his cheek. "On the contrary,

my sweet, I married you because you didn't want to get away!"

The dream was like a heavy weight on her chest, interfering with her breathing. She had always known it would be like this, that Marika wouldn't care that she was in love with Hendrik. If she wanted him, she'd take him—as she'd taken so much else from Michal in the past.

Marika had remarkably few clothes on, and what she wore revealed far more than what was hidden. Michal was ashamed for her, though she couldn't imagine why. She had seen the Dutch girl stark-naked more times than she could count. Only this time it was different. This time Hendrik was being asked to choose between them, and it was bound to be Marika, who spoke his own language, and who came from the same village as his mother and Tante Willy—

Michal was shaken awake and found that Hendrik was standing over her with the light on.

"What's the matter?" he asked. "Why are you crying?"

She turned over on her stomach and shut her eyes tight. "I'm not crying!" She tried to put him off. "I was dreaming. A silly dream it was, too."

He switched the light off again and lay down beside her, putting his arms about her.

"Marika?" he suggested softly.

"I told you it was silly! I'm sorry I woke you up."

He was silent for a minute, his hands lightly

caressing her. "Michal, you little fool, are you jealous of her?"

"I'm not jealous of anyone!" she denied sharply. "It's just that some people always succeed in getting their own way. They're not constrained by the same morality as the rest of us. Sometimes I wish I were more like that."

Hendrik laughed out loud. "Women are no judges in these matters!" he teased her. "You can believe me when I tell you that your combination of availability and disapproval has a style all its own. It's irresistible, as I'll shortly prove to you—if you don't go back to sleep!"

Michal was half-asleep already. She had never thought she would be adding kindness to Hendrik's other virtues, but it was kind to make her think he enjoyed making love to her. Or perhaps it was only the good manners he thought a husband ought to show to his wife. It was more likely that, she told herself soberly, for Hendrik was too proud a man to leave his manners behind at the bedroom door. She'd be fooling herself if she thought it was anything more than that.

Marika arrived with a flourish in the middle of Belle's preparations for her annual almsgiving. It was left to Michal to welcome her, to carry her luggage into the house, and to make up a bed for her in the smaller of the two spare rooms, because she was still using the larger one as a workroom for making her jewellery.

"Hullo, Marika," Michal said quietly, paying the

taxi driver with Hendrik's money, because, as usual, Marika didn't seem to have any.

The Dutch girl's nostrils flared angrily. "You might have come to meet me. I'm exhausted from having to drive all that long way. How far is it?"

"Forty miles." Forty miles to Paradise, as far as Michal was concerned, for there never would be any other Paradise for her but Hendrik's house.

Marika flung herself into a chair on the verandah. "Sit down, do!" she exclaimed irritably. "You know how much I hate people standing over me!"

Michal sat. "I haven't much time," she began to explain. "Things will be easier to-morrow—"

Marika turned her head and stared at Michal, without any expression that Michal could detect at all. Her eyes were cold and hard and totally without humour. The contours of her face were really very like Tante Willy's—they were as alike as two peas in a pod! It wasn't a particularly interesting face in repose; rather, it was flat and colourless, with eyes like sucked boiled sweets. Yet Marika still managed to have that something, quite impossible to define, which caught and held the attention of everyone about her, even in competition with women far more lovely than herself.

She smiled, her expression remaining as chilly as ever. "Now," she said, "it's time for you to give Hendrik back to me."

Michal managed a smile. "Really?"

"He was only on loan, you know. You did know that, didn't you?"

"You flung us together!" Michal said.

"I thought a brief affair would do you good." Marika showed her teeth in another unfriendly smile. "It was about time you came down onto the same level as the rest of us and stopped being so superior every time I met a man I liked. But I never meant for you to have rich Hendrik all to yourself for keeps! Hendrik is mine!"

"What about Joost?"

"A passing attraction—nothing more!"

"You haven't even met Hendrik—"

"I don't have to, my dear. I've seen his bank balance, which is more than enough for me. What's he like? Don't tell me you're human enough to have fallen for him?"

"I'm married to him! I sent you a telegram—"

Marika looked at her reflectively. "Are you, now? That is a trifle awkward. Never mind, my pet, I'll rescue you somehow."

"I don't want to be rescued!"

"Of course you do," Marika continued blandly. "Why else would you have sent me a telegram asking me to rescue you from a fate worse than death?"

Michal had never been more glad to see Hendrik in her life than she was when he came out onto the verandah to join them. She could hardly see him for the unshed tears that rushed into her eyes at the sight at him, but his solid, reassuring presence was something very beautiful to her.

"This . . . this is Marika," she said lamely.

If he smiles at her, she thought, *I'll know he likes her, and what will I do then?*

"I'd have known you anywhere," Hendrik said to Marika.

"I'm glad I fullfil your expectations. It must have been a nasty shock when Michal walked off the aeroplane in my place."

"It was a shock," he amended, "though not in the way you mean."

"Never mind. I'm here now," Marika went on complacently. "We'll get things sorted out in no time. Michal always does as she's told."

"Does she?" Hendrik's face was impossible to read.

Marika smiled her wide smile. "You see," she said, "I know Michal. She'd never take anything of mine."

"Not if it's really yours," Hendrik agreed pleasantly. "What kept you in Holland so long?"

"The Netherlands," Marika snapped, going on in a sexy, husky voice Michal had never heard from her before. "I had to stay in the Netherlands to see Joost settled. You do understand, darling, don't you?" She peeked up at him, inviting his laughter, rattling off some further remarks in Dutch.

Hendrik's eyes rested fleetingly on his wife's set face. "Belle was looking for you, Michal, and so was I. Where have you been all day?"

"Helping out." Michal wished she could have made some claim to have been doing something of overwhelming importance. It would have been nice to have looked as though she were an integral part of Hendrik's household, not just a hanger-on. "What did you want?"

His eyes shone green with laughter. "What do you think?"

Marika looked from one to the other of them. "Show me to my room, Michal," she commanded imperiously. "I'm sure this Belle can manage without you for a few more minutes."

"But can I?" asked Hendrik. He put a hand on the nape of Michal's neck, rubbing his fingers into her hair. He turned back to Marika, still smiling. "You may know the Michal she shows to the world, shy and biddable."

"You should have known her parents!" Marika interrupted impatiently. "They explain all there is to know about Michal! Did you know they were old enough to be her grandparents?"

"Yes," said Hendrik, "I did." His laughter rang round the verandah. "But if that's all you know about Michal, you don't know her very well. Don't let that disapproving air of hers fool you—"

"Hendrik, be quiet!"

Both he and Marika stared at Michal in open disbelief. Michal picked herself off her chair with dignity and walked away from them into the house. If he and Marika found it such fun to discuss her, they could jolly well do it behind her back! She refused to stay and listen to them.

Chapter Ten

"What a peculiar little boy!"

Michal's patience, already worn thin, rent with an expletive she had never thought to hear from her own lips. She and Marika faced each other with a mutual sense of shock.

"He's not in the least peculiar," Michal managed to say more calmly. "He's *special,* which is something quite different. He's hoping to enter a monastery next year."

"And his mother will allow it?" Marika was scandalised. "They're both peculiar! Who ever heard of a ten-year-old monk?"

"It isn't quite the same as being a Christian monk," Michal explained uncomfortably, "though we had children, boys and girls, becoming religious in the Middle Ages, and probably for much the same reasons. Saman will get a very good education, and if he doesn't like it, he can always leave when he's grown up—or before."

"But he's half-European!"

Michal had never thought of Saman as being half-anything; he was just Saman, and unique in her experience.

"What's that got to do with anything?" Michal demanded. "Not that it's any of our business, but I think he's very lucky. Belle loves him enough to let him do the one thing he wants to do. If anything goes wrong, he has Hendrik behind him, too."

Marika eyed Michal suspiciously, her mouth turned down, as if the taste of her thoughts were bitter. "I believe you're really enjoying yourself in this ghastly household! Well, enjoy it while you can, my dear! There are going to be a lot of changes when I take over, I can tell you! Tante Willy will have to go back to the Netherlands, for a start. I'm not going to have her watching everything I do and reporting back to my parents. And then there's Belle. She'll have to learn her proper place if she stays. I don't approve of servants hanging about the house when they've got nothing to do—"

"Belle isn't a servant!" Michal responded furiously. "She's Hendrik's cousin and Hans' widow. She does most of the work, it's true, but that doesn't make her anybody's servant! Why don't you try helping her to-day of all days? It's a very special day for her to-day."

Marika shrugged. "I thought you were doing that. Is that tea tray for Tante Willy, or are we actually going to be able to sit down and have a cosy chat together over a cup of tea?"

"It's for Tante Willy!" Michal said. Then she went out of the room, banging the door shut behind her.

Tante Willy, to everyone's surprise, had taken a deep and lasting dislike for Marika. Michal suspected she could sense that the Dutch girl had no sympathy for the disabled, or for anyone else who got between her and the life-style she wanted for herself. It must have been a particularly sour disappointment to Tante Willy. She had so longed to have someone from her own village to talk to and to take the place of the sister she had sparred with all her life, until more then half her family had been taken away from her in the helicopter crash.

"I thought you'd forgotten all about me," the Dutch woman sniffed as Michal knocked on her door. "How's that unpleasant young woman?"

Michal put down the tray and wiped the sweat from her brow. "Please don't," she said. "Marika is a friend of mine."

"Is she? Don't be more stupid than you can help, my girl! You may be her friend, but she's no friend of yours!"

"Tante Willy—"

But nothing was going to stop the older woman. "The trouble with you is that you can't see farther than the end of your nose! Tell Marika to go, and let's be comfortable again. Or are you going to let her break up your marriage and take Hendrik away from you? I find it extremely irritating that you should do so little to help yourself! Just like Hen-

157

drik's mother! She put up with me meddling with her marriage for years! But even she wasn't as unselfish as you pretend to be. She made sure of her man before she tested his loyalty with me, not afterwards!"

"I wouldn't be such a fool as to put Hendrik to any test!" Michal denied, hanging onto the shreds of her temper with increasing difficulty.

"Oh? Then what are you doing? Why is that girl still here?"

"Hendrik—"

Tante Willy's neigh of laughter caught Michal on the raw. "Have you thought that *he* might be testing *you*?"

Michal turned on her. "It's none of your business if he is!" she declared violently.

"No, but I like you better than I thought I would," Tante Willy confessed cheerfully.

Michal sat down on the edge of Tante Willy's bed. Why would Hendrik want to test her loyalty to him? She wasn't the one who had forced him into a loveless marriage and who now regretted it, having met Marika! On the contrary, she thought she was behaving remarkably well under the circumstances. She hadn't rebuked him by word or deed, nor even pointed out that she had told him this would happen, that all men always had preferred Marika to herself. She had had sufficient self-respect to insist on moving back to her own room last night, but she had even explained that away by saying she had wanted to get to work on her engagement ring.

And Hendrik hadn't cared. All he had said was,

"What will you do if I do take up Marika's offer while you're away doing your own thing?"

"What offer?" she had asked him, feeling sick.

"What offer d'you suppose!" he had retorted.

But she hadn't been testing him in any way! She truly hadn't! She had known from the very beginning that he would welcome Marika with open arms, married to her or not! It had been no surprise to her that he showed no sign of wanting the Dutch girl to go.

Her thoughts returning to the present, Michal mumbled to Tante Willy, "Like me or not, you may not have me here much longer. Marika was Hendrik's first choice."

"He hadn't seen you then!"

And now he probably wished he hadn't! Michal stood up again, remembering something else she had meant to say.

"Tante Willy, Belle's holding her almsgiving this morning, and Marika doesn't approve of Hendrik having to pay for all the food. Will you try to keep her out of the way for an hour or two? Talk to her about Holland—"

"Can't you find anything for her to do?"

"No, I can't! And I haven't time to take her out anywhere. With twenty-five men to feed, all of them with excellent appetites, there hasn't been time to do anything, except cook and get ready for the invasion! I wonder why there must be twenty-five of them!"

"It's a good, solid number," Tante Willy suggested. "Twenty-five is the minimum. If there aren't enough living in the monastery, they bring in others from the surrounding shrines to make up the numbers. But why they do anything they do, I've never bothered to enquire!"

Michal poured out a cup of tea and handed it to the Dutch woman. "Saman will know. He's in his element, helping us get everything ready. He's been a great help, too. I shouldn't have liked to have had to prepare all those vegetables on my own, nor have rushed back and forth to the monastery to borrow their pots and pans because ours simply aren't large enough!"

"Our pots and pans?"

Michal flushed. "In a manner of speaking, they are."

Tante Willy saw her turn to go. "However busy you are, my dear, surely you can spare a couple of minutes to chat with me? I'm as much an object for your charity as any of those monks!"

"No, you're not—you're family!" Michal protested indignantly.

"Marika doesn't think so," Tante Willy pointed out dryly. "Which reminds me, I haven't given you a wedding present yet. It isn't easy to get anything you'd like when you're tied to the house, as I am, so I'm going to give you my own dower chest, which I brought with me when I came here to be married. It was my mother's before it was mine, and for all I know, it might have been her mother's, too."

Michal twisted her fingers together. "Are you sure you want me to have it? I don't come from your village—"

"I wouldn't be giving it to you if I didn't!" Tante

Willy told her crossly. "Do what you like with it! Sell it if you like, only don't argue with me about it! Have you ever heard of sgraffito ware?"

Michal shook her head. "What is it?"

"You must know sgraffito tableware! Very pretty! With the design scratched on the surface through a coating of glaze. I thought you knew about all such things!"

"Only jewellery," Michal said apologetically.

"Well, I'm giving you that, too, together with some slipware that you'll like better than anything else. It has birds and tulips on it. I remember seeing it being made as a child. They do it freehand, dripping it directly onto the moulded clay through a spout. The tulips are rather like the ones on your ring."

So Tante Willy had noticed the pattern on her wedding ring. "It's very kind of you," Michal began.

"It's in my own interests, if you want to know! Someone has to persuade you that you really are Mrs. van der Aa!"

"Yes. Well, I must go," Michal said in a hurry. "I promised Belle I wouldn't be long. She needs all the help she can get! Shall I send Marika in to you for a visit?"

"If you must," Tante Willy sighed, momentarily defeated.

The long line of saffron-robed monks came slowly up the drive. Some of them were carrying the old-fashioned oval fans that Michal thought to be so pretty. Others had succumbed to modern life sufficiently to carry large black umbrellas, instead. They were a cheerful lot. Everyone, it seemed, enjoyed almsgiving days, both donors and recipients. There was a party spirit in the air, and Saman wasn't the only one who was scarlet-faced with pleasure at the sight of their arrival.

Michal, now that most of the hard work was done, would have retired and left Belle to her moment of triumph, but Saman vetoed this with a firmness that was quite unexpected in one of his tender age.

"The abbot will speak to you after he's eaten," he told Michal in a solemn voice. "It's a great honour. He'll help you get things sorted out."

Michal gaped at him. "And how will that help?"

"Mother asked him to make out your chart the day you were married. He can tell you lots of things you won't know about yourself."

When Saman introduced Michal to the ancient abbot, she was glad she had stayed. The old man put the palms of his hands together and raised them up to a pair of twinkling black eyes.

"Welcome to Sri Lanka, Mrs. van der Aa." He gestured to the ground beside him. "I hope you find yourself happily married. Your chart was favourable to the union."

Michal bowed her head, seating herself with care a little distance away from him. Holy men didn't care to be too close to women, and she had no desire to offend this charming old man.

"I'm a Christian. I don't really believe in such things," Michal told him.

"Of course not. You believe in charity, though, I see, or you wouldn't have spent so much of your time helping Belle to make this meal for us. Her husband was a Christian, also, yet his death is marked in this very Buddhist way because he married a Buddhist. Cause and effect, my dear lady. None of us can escape this law of life, whatever we profess to believe."

"I think we make our own happiness," Michal said slowly.

"That's what I'm saying," the old man agreed. "Don't leave it too late and store up unhappiness for you and Hendrik, instead. We can't always avoid action, much as we'd like to do so. Cause and effect," the abbot repeated. "None of us can escape it, and the wisest amongst us draw strength from it. Good actions bring about good results—try it and see!"

Michal left him soon after that, aware that there must be many others who would take the opportunity to seek his advice. She bowed to him again and slipped away from the crowded room to think over what he had said to her.

Going out the front door, she almost tripped over the rows of sandals that had been left there by the monks. She had thought they only removed their shoes on going into a holy place, not somewhere as commonplace as an ordinary house. The gesture touched her and she warmed to these highly educated, sophisticated men, who chose to live such a simple life, hidden away in the countryside, as far away as was possible from the fashionable seats of learning and the famous shrines that grew rich on the many pilgrims who visited them.

The bee-eaters were again flitting over the slow-moving water of the river in their search for food. The green of their bodies flashed in the sunlight, making Michal conscious of how much they had become a symbol to her of all she longed for in Sri Lanka. She stood for a long moment, watching them, glad of the silence, and happy that she was alone to enjoy their beauty.

Cause and effect. Afterwards, she couldn't have said the exact moment when everything had fallen into place for her. All she knew was that it had, and it was so simple that she wondered how she could possibly have overlooked it before. She had been confused and at a loss ever since she had arrived in place of Marika, but now she saw the inevitability of her position and her heart flooded with happiness. It was simple. All that was needed was for Marika to go away.

Yes, Marika had to go, not because she was any threat to Michal, but because she had succeeded in making a disturbance in the household that was Michal's responsibility. She had made Tante Willy feel insecure, she had patronised Belle, and she thought Saman peculiar. Michal could afford to be tolerant of one of her oldest friends, but not if the cost was to be borne by her new family.

Hendrik had married *her,* Michal Brent, and that was the cause of everything she had to do now. She was Mrs. Hendrik van der Aa, not Marika, and not his dead fiancée, no matter how much Hendrik had loved her. For all she knew, she might already be carrying the seed of Hendrik's child within her, for neither of them had done anything to prevent her from conceiving on the occasions they had made love together.

What was more, if she was Hendrik's wife, she was entitled to share his bed, Marika or no Marika. She had been a fool to take herself off in a huff because she'd been too insecure and too immature to see what had to be done before. She would move her things back straight away and be done with it. After that, she would cope with Marika. She faced up to the prospect with a certain relish that amused her. Cause and effect, she thought. Really, it was no more than common sense!

Tante Willy's dower chest had been dumped in Michal's bedroom, looking exotic and out of place amongst the jeweller's instruments, pieces of silver, and scattered gems with which Michal had surrounded herself. Tante Willy had been the older sister, Michal remembered, and was all the more touched that she should have given such a valuable part of her heritage away to her.

She thought the chest very beautiful as she went down on her knees before it and opened up the stiff locks, intrigued to know what she would find inside. She found the slipware almost immediately and sat on the floor, hugging it to her as though it were the most valuable thing in the world. The birds were as vividly green as she could have wished, and the tulips exactly as she had expected them to be. Every time she looked at them, she would see Hendrik's

watchful gaze and that light in his eyes they sometimes held just before he kissed her. She took a plate
in her hand and touched the bright colours with the
tips of her fingers, her mind and heart full of her love
for Hendrik.

She would go at once and thank Tante Willy for
the gift. There were no words with which to express
her pleasure in receiving the slipware, but she
thought the Dutch woman would understand. The
relationship between Hendrik's mother and her sister hadn't been as one-sided as Michal had thought.
Tante Willy had a lot to give under that astringent
manner of hers. She was like Marika in that, too, as
well as in looks. Marika had often been kind, in a
careless sort of way, when Michal had found herself
completely alone after both her parents had died.

Marika shot to her feet like a jack-in-the-box
when Michal came into Tante Willy's room.

"Where have you been?" she snapped at Michal.

"Opening my wedding present," Michal answered
calmly. She went over to the bed and hugged Tante
Willy with enthusiasm. "It's the most beautiful thing
I've ever seen! I'll never be able to thank you
properly for it!"

Tante Willy was characteristically terse in her
response. "Save it for Hendrik," she advised. "He
won't like you thinking it to be better than the
sapphire he gave you!"

Michal grinned. "I haven't made it into a ring yet.
I ought to get on with it, but there hasn't been much
time to-day."

"What sapphire?" Marika demanded.

166

"He gave it to me for an engagement ring," Michal told her. "I'll show you, if you like."

Marika was glad of anything that released her from the company of Tante Willy.

"If you'd left me with that old witch any longer, I'd have gone mad!" she exclaimed as soon as they'd gained the corridor.

Michal flashed her friend a smile. "Don't you like her?"

"Does anyone?"

Michal nodded. "I do."

"Surprising," Marika remarked. "I should have thought you'd be scared stiff of her."

Michal opened her bedroom door with a flourish. "Because you are?"

Marika was visibly shaken. "You've changed—"

"Yes," Michal agreed with satisfaction. "I was a bit confused before, especially by your arrival after you'd given me to understand you were going to marry Joost—"

"*Marry* Joost? You must be mad. Joost was all right for a mild fling, but he's as penniless as most students of his age. I mean to marry money and a pleasant, secure future!"

"That's what Tante Willy said you'd say. She thought you'd sent me out here to keep Hendrik amused until you'd had enough of Joost and were ready to settle down."

"I haven't changed my mind about that!" Marika said darkly.

"No, but circumstances have changed," Michal said gently. "Hendrik married me—"

"A marriage that can be annulled!"

Michal shook her head. "I'm sorry, but it can't be. I'm Mrs. Hendrik van der Aa, and that's the way I'm staying. Really, I can't thank you enough for sending me out here in your stead, though, at first, I thought I'd rather die than be married out of hand because I was the only convenient female round."

"You could have said no," Marika pointed out.

"How? I didn't even have my fare home. I was stuck here, and that was the price Hendrik demanded for your non-arrival. You were the fairy godmother who waved her wand and arranged my marriage for me. Fortunately, I'm very much in love with Hendrik—"

"He isn't with you!"

That hurt, but Michal managed to ignore it. "He married me. He insisted on marrying me—and neither you, nor I, can alter that. In fact, when you think about it, I think you'll see it's the best thing that could have happened. You don't really want to live outside Europe, and Sri Lanka is a long, long way from the Netherlands. What would you do here, disliking everyone in the house, and the climate even more? This isn't your scene; it's mine."

Marika flung herself into the only vacant chair, looking about her with distaste. The slipware caught her eyes and she visibly shuddered.

"How vulgar can you get? Is that Tante Willy's wedding present?"

"Yes. D'you want to see the sapphire Hendrik gave me?"

Marika took the stone from Michal, her pale eyes hardening into a look of sheer longing. "I'll make a bargain with you," Marika said at last. "Make the sapphire into a ring for me and I'll take the next plane back to the Netherlands. You won't miss it! There'll be lots of other stones for you, but I'll never own anything comparable! You owe it to me, Michal! You know you do!"

Did she? But was it hers to give away? Michal chewed thoughtfully on her lower lip. "You won't like the setting I'd planned for it," she compromised.

"Then change it to something I do like! You haven't made it up yet."

"I'll think about it," Michal said.

"It's the only way you'll get me to go away," Marika gloated, sure she was going to get her own way.

"I'll ask Hendrik," Michal murmured reluctantly.

"Ask Hendrik what?"

Michal nearly jumped out of her skin. She turned and saw her husband in the doorway. The sight of him turned her bones to water. She wondered if she'd ever find the courage to tell him how much she loved him, but then, perhaps, he already knew.

It was Marika who answered him. "Michal is going to make the sapphire into a ring for me. It'll be something for me to take back to the Netherlands with me, as I'm not wanted here."

"Was that Michal's idea?"

"Of course not! But surely you're not going to deprive me of a small souvenir of my visit!"

Hendrik shrugged. "It's Michal's ring."

Marika got leisurely to her feet and drifted towards the open door. "Good. I find there's nothing else I want here, unless you were to offer me a diamond of comparable value."

Michal's glance faltered under the green of Hendrik's. She wiped the palms of her hands nervously on the legs of her trousers.

"Look what Tante Willy's given us for a wedding present," she said at last.

But Hendrik went on looking at her. "Are you going to give away your sapphire?"

"She won't go, otherwise!"

Hendrik's hands came down on her shoulders. He turned her face up to his, his fingers pressing painfully on her chin.

"If you want my help, you'll have to ask for it," he told her brutally.

She took a deep, gasping breath. "I can manage by myself!" she claimed.

"Can you?" He cast a comprehensive look round the room. "It looks like it! You haven't left yourself much room to sleep, have you?"

"Because I don't sleep in here anymore," she told him haughtily. "I sleep with my husband, where I belong!"

"If you really mean that," Hendrik said, "it would be worth a diamond to send Marika reeling back to Holland! But you didn't think of that last night, did you?"

Michal's cheeks were scarlet, but she refused to look away. "I'd forgotten who I was last night," she said grandly.

He was very still. "Oh? And who are you?"

Michal drew herself up to her full height. "Mrs. Hendrik van der Aa!"

Chapter Eleven

Michal had finished the ring. She put it in the palm of her hand, examining it carefully from every angle. It happened so seldom—she would have said it never happened at all—that the finished article was better than her first vision of what it might turn out to be. It had happened with this ring. It was the most beautiful thing she had ever made. The jewel was perfectly shown off by the heavy silver setting.

She put the ring in her pocket and stretched her aching back. The time had gone so quickly, she hadn't realised that the sun was already dropping from the sky, signalling the end of the day. It was more than time that she went to help Belle clear up the kitchen. She would offer to cook the dinner, she thought, and make a special occasion of it. The thought made her blush, for she couldn't deceive herself that what she was actually waiting for was after dinner, when she would be alone with Hendrik once again.

Belle, tired but happy after the success of her alms-giving, was only too glad to relinquish the kitchen to Michal as soon as she'd finished washing up.

"Did you speak to the abbot, Michal?" Belle asked shyly, as she washed the last of the enormous pans they had borrowed from the local monastery for the occasion.

"I spoke to lots of people," Michal answered cautiously.

Belle smiled. "I'm glad. You sound as though you mean dinner to-night to be a special occasion. Sure you don't want any help?"

Michal shook her head. "You must be dropping, as it is. If I need any help, I'll ask Marika."

"That'll be the day!"

Michal laughed out loud. "Marika is a very good cook," she declared. "In fact, she has all the domestic skills when she wants to use them. Her parents saw to that!"

Belle wrinkled up her nose. "She has a practical nature. Yours is warmly romantic. She wouldn't have helped me this morning!"

"No," Michal agreed soberly. She grinned suddenly. "How d'you know I didn't help you only because I'm Mrs. van der Aa and it was expected of me?"

Belle looked suddenly like her son. "Because this morning you didn't know you were a van der Aa," she said gently. "To-night you do, and I'm glad for you. You're exactly the right wife for Hendrik to have! I hope he's told you so by now."

Michal hesitated. "What about the girl who died?"

"She was pretty," Belle acknowledged. "She liked parties and pretty clothes and having a good time. She was very young. Mr. Hendrik had already found that out before the helicopter crash. It was a bad day for all of us, but worse for him. He felt guilty that he didn't miss her more."

"I think he loved her," Michal said.

"She was there to be loved."

Michal sighed. "Like me?"

Belle laughed easily. "Mr. Hendrik must tell you that for himself. What are you going to cook for to-night?"

Michal didn't know. She decided to consult Tante Willy and found the Dutch woman to be surprisingly helpful. She knew all the dishes that had been Hendrik's favourites as a boy; more than that, she was prepared to allow herself to be carried into the kitchen so that she could oversee the cooking to make sure that everything was done as she thought it ought to be.

With the meal in the oven, Michal turned her attention to the table, using the slipware dishes Tante Willy had given her. She found herself mooning over the dishes, dreaming over the birds and the tulips and seeing only Hendrik's face in their depths.

After that, she had only to dress herself. She put on the scarlet silk dress she had worn for her wedding. It was an unusual choice for someone of her colouring to choose, but it was the most dramatic dress she had; it set her copper-coloured hair on fire and accentuated the hazel-brown of her eyes. She made up her face with a lavish hand, knowing as she did it that her motives were mixed. She didn't only want to impress Hendrik; *she wanted to outshine Marika,* to put the other girl so far in the shade that Hendrik van der Aa would only have eyes for his wife.

She took a last look at herself in the mirror and then stood up, taking a deep breath to give herself courage. At the same moment, the door opened behind her and Hendrik came in. He was dressed in a dinner jacket and looked so fine in formal dress that the sight of him took her breath away.

"What are you doing in here?" Hendrik asked her. "I thought you were moving back in with me."

"I am." Michal gave him a look that was both shy and eager. "Just for to-night, though, I wanted to dress by myself." She searched round for her discarded jeans. "By the way," she said, "I've finished the ring. D'you want to see it?" She lowered her eyes to the middle stud in his gleaming white shirt. "How did you know we were having a special dinner to-night?"

"Belle told me. And, yes, I do want to see the ring."

She held it out for his inspection. "I haven't tried it on yet," she confessed. "I wanted to know what you thought of it first."

It was terribly important that he should like it.

"Do you like it?" The words caught in Michal's throat, betraying her anxiety. "Do you?"

"There are no roses on it," Hendrik said.

Her eyes swept up to his. "No, because we're not exchanging rings this time. The tulips are there, though, and . . . and birds."

"So I see. Why the birds? Are they meant to be symbolic of Sri Lanka?"

She shook her head, the colour rising in her cheeks. "They're bee-eaters. They remind me of you because they're the same green colour as your eyes." The words ran together in her hurry to get them out. "They're on the plates Tante Willy has given us, too!"

"Bee-eaters?"

"Green birds!"

"I wonder why we've never seen these plates before," he said.

"They were Tante Willy's."

Hendrik dropped the ring into his pocket without further comment. He held out his arm to Michal in a courtly gesture that in anyone else would have embarrassed her.

"Shall we go in to dinner?" he invited her.

Michal patted her hair into shape, oblivious of the fact she had only just finished arranging it. She felt hollow inside when she thought of the ordeal before her. What if Hendrik didn't want her, after all?

"I'm cook as well as hostess," she reminded him. "We're going to have a family dinner to round out Belle's day."

"A nice treat for her," he approved. "How did her almsgiving go?"

"Exhausting! But I enjoyed it very much. It was such a pretty sight when they all arrived in a long, saffron-coloured line. They looked too handsome to be monks."

His eyes were lazy and very green. "Trying to make me jealous, Michal?" Hendrik challenged her.

She hadn't even thought of it as a possibility until that moment. "Could I?" she asked curiously.

"I don't share what is mine," he said.

She opened her mouth to tell him not to be so pompous, but he had already taken her arm in his and was walking her with determination towards the dining room. She still might have made some protest at being consigned to being no more than his chattel, but he took her down the full length of the table and seated her in the hostess' chair, a seat she never would have taken for herself, with so much amusement in his smile that she was quite overcome and too shy to say anything at all.

Marika was looking less than her best, seated beside Tante Willy. It was obvious that the sight of Saman and his mother on the other side of the table distressed her, the more so when the boy insisted on eating only his usual vegetarian fare.

"He ought to be made to eat what's put in front of him!" Marika announced to the table at large.

"Why?" Michal asked, laughing. "It must bring me more merit to give him something he wants to eat. I need all the merit I can get."

Marika looked cross. "What will you do with it when you have it?"

"Keep up with Hendrik," Michal said slowly. "Saman is already too advanced for me."

Marika looked round the table, her eyes hard. "Speaking for myself," she said, "I shan't be sorry to get back to the Netherlands and normal people! You're welcome to your pot of gold, Miss Michal Brent. You'll have earned every penny of it before you're through."

Hendrik snapped out of his lethargy. "Michal van der Aa," he corrected, an edge to his voice that made Michal quiver with an inward excitement. He put his hand in his pocket and drew out Michal's ring and an envelope. He passed the sealed envelope over to Marika. "That'll make you and my wife all square."

Marika ripped it open, allowing the diamond inside to fall out onto the table in front of her. For a moment she looked at it in silence. Then, her eyes round with astonishment, she turned to Hendrik.

"Michal doesn't owe me anything," Marika said awkwardly. "You must want her pretty badly to pay so much for her!"

"I do!"

Michal was furiously angry. "You don't have to buy me, Hendrik van der Aa! I'm not for sale!"

Marika breathed a light laugh. "He doesn't have to buy you. Anyone with half an eye can see you're head-over-heels in love with him. You always were a fool, Michal. If you'd played your cards better, you could have had the diamond, as well as the sapphire!"

Hendrik's lip curled with contempt. "Leave Michal alone, Marika," he advised her coldly. "Attend to your own business—Joost Janssen, or whoever it happens to be—and leave Michal to me! Take your diamond and go!"

Michal left the table and went into the kitchen. How could he do this to her? What had she done to him that he should deliberately humiliate her at her own dinner party?

She looked up from the meat she was frying in the Dutch style when Belle followed her flight from the dining room.

"Did Mr. Hendrik tell you he asked me to move your things back into his room?" Belle asked.

Michal envied her her gentle dignity. "It isn't only Marika," she said. "I can't forget he really wanted to marry someone else."

Belle tied an apron over her sarong and took over the frying pan, her features relaxing into a wide smile.

"Michal, you are so foolish! Ask Mr. Hendrik to tell you about his romance with Julia sometime. She was a flower for a man to wear in his lapel and enjoy the envy of his fellows. Poor girl, she was never anything more than that!"

Michal didn't believe her. She piled the meat up high on a warmed plate, then put Saman's vegetable stew out on another plate, making it look as attractive as she was able.

"We'd better go back," Michal said on a sigh. "Thanks for your help, Belle. This was meant to be an evening off for you."

"There will be other evenings," Belle said comfortably. "To-night must be for you and Mr. Hendrik."

"With Marika looking on?"

"Since when did you mind children playing with

their toys round your feet?" Belle rebuked her as she picked up her son's vegetable stew and returned to the dining room.

Michal followed Belle slowly, dreading having to make small talk with Marika and Hendrik. She needn't have worried, for Tante Willy was in full spate as she took her seat again.

"Hurry up, do, both of you! Can't you see I'm getting tired and need my food? It's my favourite, and I mean to eat a great deal of it." She glared round the table. "And I'll have coffee to-night, no matter what any of you say! I'm sick of the endless tea we drink all the time. Coffee I want, and coffee I mean to have!"

Michal looked down the long length of the table, seeking her ring, but it was nowhere to be seen. Hendrik must have put it back in his pocket. Perhaps he wasn't going to give it to her, after all. Perhaps he thought she'd think it was payment for services rendered, too. Tears flooded into her eyes and she blinked them away. What an endless day it had been!

Michal went to her own bedroom out of habit. At least, that's what she told herself. Actually, she didn't know what else to do with herself. She felt that she couldn't go off to Hendrik's room and undress there. Of course, she had the right—she had all the rights and privileges that being Mrs. van der Aa gave her, like sitting in the chair of the lady of the house opposite Hendrik at table. The carved arms, bright with the polish of centuries, would have given most occupants a rare satisfaction, she had no doubt.

She had felt like a small child dressed up for the day in her mother's clothes, strutting about in high-heeled shoes several sizes too big for her.

"Still hiding, Michal?"

She jumped and turned to face Hendrik, her eyes wide. "I was tidying up," she explained. "I was working in here all afternoon—"

"Tidying up?" he asked dryly.

It was just her luck, she thought, to be caught at such a moment, studying the star-spangled heavens and the silver ball of the still-full moon. The stars seemed much nearer in Sri Lanka than they did in Europe. If she put out a hand, she could almost touch them—only in real life they were as far away as ever!

"Dinner wasn't much fun, after all, was it?"

Hendrik joined Michal by the window. "Tante Willy did her best for you."

"Yes, bless her." She stared resolutely out at the black velvet sky. "She hasn't as much in common with Marika as she thought she'd have. She can't understand that Marika's never enjoyed wearing national costume and being a sideshow for tourists. Tante Willy loved her village, didn't she?"

"She left it quickly enough when the opportunity came—as did my mother. Marriage was the only way they could escape. Things are different now."

"Only you don't believe it," she accused him. "You still think of women as things to be managed, and pampered, and kept severely in their proper place!"

He was amused. "Do I?"

"You know you do! If you didn't, you never would

have agreed to have had some woman you'd never seen sent out here to be your wife! Nor would you have given me no choice but to be married off to you, as if I had no feelings or ambitions of my own—none that mattered! I'm not a real person to you at all!"

"My dear girl, you haven't the faintest idea of how real you are to me! You knocked me for six—"

Her giggle brought a frown to his face. "We play cricket in Sri Lanka," he told her loftily. "I play quite well myself." His frown deepened. "What's so funny in that?"

She didn't know. She certainly couldn't have told him. "Did Julia watch you play cricket?" she asked him deliberately. He'd look very well in white flannel trousers, she thought irrelevantly. It was something in the way he wore his clothes.

The look he gave her was sharp enough to hurt. "What do you want to know about Julia?"

Michal bit her lip. "Do you still think about her? Did you love her very much? Things like that."

He put an arm round her shoulders, his body warm against hers. "I used to think about her," he admitted. "I used to wonder why I didn't miss her more than I did. She was a very nice person and she didn't deserve to die. I was distressed about the waste. I even thought I loved her, until something happened to make me see that I never had loved her, nor any other woman."

"I don't think that's true," Michal objected. "You know a lot about women, too much not to have had a great deal to do with them! You play us like fishes on a hook!"

His laughter undermined her hard-won advantage. "And you don't?" he retorted. His face softened. "My dear little Michal, you haven't the least idea of the impact you made on us all with your arrival, have you?"

"*Me?*"

His arms went about her in the most satisfactory manner. "Sometimes, just sometimes, I thought you knew."

She peeped at him through her lashes, as shy of him as she had ever been. She tried to explain. "It was like being taken over by a stranger, a *wanton* stranger, who liked being married to you very much. I was afraid of her. To-day, I realised she was only me, after all. I like being married to you, too."

His kisses were warm and gentle. "Are you ready to come to bed?" he whispered in her ear.

She nodded, dropping her head onto his broad shoulder. "You haven't given me my ring yet," she reminded him.

Hendrik put her away from him with a sigh. "I'll give it to you after I've told you about Julia. I've something else to tell you before I put it on your finger. I wasn't going to tell you. I thought you'd run away back to England if I did, but, somehow or other, my home has become your home, hasn't it? You don't mind sharing it with the others, do you?"

Michal was astonished that he should ask. "It's their home, too!" she reproached him with a touch of indignation.

"Marika wouldn't see it that way!"

Michal was obliged to acknowledge the justice of that. Marika didn't like any of them. She would never be able to see that Tante Willy's astringent manner hid a warm heart, or that Belle and Saman were human beings, just like herself.

"She's always said she hated the village where she came from," Michal remembered, "but she'll never be happy away from it. I've never had any roots anywhere else, so it's much easier for me. Marika doesn't mean half of what she says. She can be very kind."

"I'll take your word for it," Hendrik said dryly. He held out a hand to her. "Come to bed, my love."

His love? She felt a warm, buttery feeling inside her and willingly put her hand in his. It was probably only a manner of speaking, but one day she would make it come true!

They walked hand in hand down the corridor to where his larger bedroom was situated. Hendrik gestured towards the bed and Michal took off her robe, sitting up against the pillows like an expectant small girl. He sat on the edge of the bed, his eyes so deep a green as they studied her face that her blood began to race with the pleasure they gave her.

"I've never been in love before," he said quietly. "Julia would have made a suitable wife, but there was never anything more to it than that. I didn't think there was a woman born who could move me almost to tears with her beauty, until I wanted her so badly I'd do anything to keep her by my side. There was never anyone like that for me, and I thought there never would be."

"Many people don't ever know a love like that," Michal said, trying to comfort him.

His smile was full of wry self-mockery. "I thought

184

I was one of them until you stepped off that plane and into my heart. I took one look at you and I was lost! The only thing that mattered to me was to prevent you from getting away again. I wanted to wake up in the mornings and see that coppery hair of yours on my pillow. I wanted to take you into my arms and make love to you until you began to feel for me a little of what I felt for you!"

"I thought you had to marry someone—"

"Tante Willy wanted me to marry. She wrote home to her village and set the whole thing in motion. I'd have found some way of sending the wretched girl home again. But not you! Even if you were frightened of me at first, you had to stay—"

"Whatever the cost?"

"I'll make it up to you, sweetheart. We have a whole lifetime ahead of us in which to teach you to love me. All you have to do is to allow yourself to enjoy the attraction between us until you can feel something more and the whole of you wants to share your whole life with me. Is that too much to ask?"

She clutched at the sheet, unable to believe that this was Hendrik speaking, a strange, unsure Hendrik who felt it necessary to plead with her for something he already had. To be sure, he'd stolen it from her, she reminded herself, but she couldn't hold it against him. It was what she had wanted, too.

"You shouldn't have forced me to marry you," she said. "Everybody has a right to some choice in what he or she wants to do. I wasn't going anywhere. It'd have taken me ages to make enough money to go back to England."

The tense look was back in his face. "I couldn't wait. Darling, don't you understand yet how much I want you?"

She pleated the sheet into a little pattern and then straightened it out again. "You took a terrible risk. You could have made me hate you—"

"Could have?"

The warmth crept up her throat and face. "I fell in love with you almost at once. Oh, Hendrik, you fool, d'you think I'd have married you otherwise? I'd have found some way of getting out of it!"

"You sent a telegram to Marika asking her help!"

Michal nodded, not looking at Hendrik. "I didn't think she'd get it, and there wasn't time for her to do anything. Even Tante Willy knew that!"

He leaned forwards, touching his lips to hers. "Tante Willy has taken a great liking to you, hasn't she? It didn't take you long to have us all at your feet. Can you be happy, for the rest of your life, here with me?"

She flung her arms round his neck and pulled him close. "I love you, I love you, *I love you!* Please make love to me!"

The fires of passion rose between them, threatening to engulf them altogether, but still Hendrik drew back. He felt in his pocket for her ring and held it out to her.

"I didn't want to give it to you until you knew how much I love you," he said. "We both put something into its creation, and that's how marriage ought to be. Will you wear it with love?"

"Always!"

He placed it on her finger, pushing it home with

hands that trembled. She looked down at it, her heart on fire with the depth of her feeling for him. She put her other hand over both of his.

"I'm glad it isn't a diamond," she said. "Diamonds have their uses"—her eyes crinkled with the beginnings of a smile—"but they're not for Mrs. van der Aa!"

They laughed together and, as suddenly, stopped, feeling for each other with a hunger that would not be denied. Her mouth opened to his as she pushed his clothes away from him and made him welcome on the bed beside her. Diamonds were a commonplace, something everyone was supposed to want and admire, but she needed something as unique as the man she was married to. The burghers made strong husbands, Tante Willy had told her, but she had said nothing of the sweetness of Hendrik's love. That was something Michal was only beginning to discover for herself, something to be savoured and lived all her life long. She thought of the long flight into the unknown she had made when she had come to Sri Lanka. Who would have thought it would have turned into a homecoming, bringing her to the only place in the world where she really belonged, Hendrik's arms?

"I love you, Hendrik van der Aa," Michal whispered, and was rewarded by the fervour with which he kissed her.

"I love you, too," he said. *"My* Michal, *my wife!"*

And she was lost once more in the green depths of his eyes, the rest of the world slipping away from her. Forty miles from Paradise? They had already been there and back again, she thought, and the fountains were clearly to be heard, bringing the waters of renewed life to them both. She put up a hand and rubbed the roughened skin of his jaw, smiling to herself. This man was Paradise enough for her!

Silhouette Romance

15-Day Free Trial Offer
6 Silhouette Romances

6 Silhouette Romances, free for 15 days! We'll send you 6 new Silhouette Romances to keep for 15 days, absolutely free! If you decide not to keep them, send them back to us. You pay nothing.

Free Home Delivery. But if you enjoy them as much as we think you will, keep them by paying the invoice enclosed with your free trial shipment. We'll pay all shipping and handling charges. You get the convenience of Home Delivery and we pay the postage and handling charge each month.

Don't miss a copy. The Silhouette Book Club is the way to make sure you'll be able to receive every new romance we publish before they're sold out. There is no minimum number of books to buy and you can cancel at any time.

Silhouette Romance

IT'S YOUR OWN SPECIAL TIME
Contemporary romances for today's women.
Each month, six very special love stories will be yours
from SILHOUETTE. Look for them wherever books are sold
or order now from the coupon below.

$1.50 each

☐ 5 Goforth	☐ 28 Hampson	☐ 54 Beckman	☐ 83 Halston
☐ 6 Stanford	☐ 29 Wildman	☐ 55 LaDame	☐ 84 Vitek
☐ 7 Lewis	☐ 30 Dixon	☐ 56 Trent	☐ 85 John
☐ 8 Beckman	☐ 32 Michaels	☐ 57 John	☐ 86 Adams
☐ 9 Wilson	☐ 33 Vitek	☐ 58 Stanford	☐ 87 Michaels
☐ 10 Caine	☐ 34 John	☐ 59 Vernon	☐ 88 Stanford
☐ 11 Vernon	☐ 35 Stanford	☐ 60 Hill	☐ 89 James
☐ 17 John	☐ 38 Browning	☐ 61 Michaels	☐ 90 Major
☐ 19 Thornton	☐ 39 Sinclair	☐ 62 Halston	☐ 92 McKay
☐ 20 Fulford	☐ 46 Stanford	☐ 63 Brent	☐ 93 Browning
☐ 22 Stephens	☐ 47 Vitek	☐ 71 Ripy	☐ 94 Hampson
☐ 23 Edwards	☐ 48 Wildman	☐ 73 Browning	☐ 95 Wisdom
☐ 24 Healy	☐ 49 Wisdom	☐ 76 Hardy	☐ 96 Beckman
☐ 25 Stanford	☐ 50 Scott	☐ 78 Oliver	☐ 97 Clay
☐ 26 Hastings	☐ 52 Hampson	☐ 81 Roberts	☐ 98 St. George
☐ 27 Hampson	☐ 53 Browning	☐ 82 Dailey	☐ 99 Camp

$1.75 each

☐ 100 Stanford	☐ 110 Trent	☐ 120 Carroll	☐ 130 Hardy
☐ 101 Hardy	☐ 111 South	☐ 121 Langan	☐ 131 Stanford
☐ 102 Hastings	☐ 112 Stanford	☐ 122 Scofield	☐ 132 Wisdom
☐ 103 Cork	☐ 113 Browning	☐ 123 Sinclair	☐ 133 Rowe
☐ 104 Vitek	☐ 114 Michaels	☐ 124 Beckman	☐ 134 Charles
☐ 105 Eden	☐ 115 John	☐ 125 Bright	☐ 135 Logan
☐ 106 Dailey	☐ 116 Lindley	☐ 126 St. George	☐ 136 Hampson
☐ 107 Bright	☐ 117 Scott	☐ 127 Roberts	☐ 137 Hunter
☐ 108 Hampson	☐ 118 Dailey	☐ 128 Hampson	☐ 138 Wilson
☐ 109 Vernon	☐ 119 Hampson	☐ 129 Converse	☐ 139 Vitek

Coming next month from
Silhouette Romances

The Dawn Is Golden by Anne Hampson

Melanie believed her only means of escape was to flee with Vidas Loudaros to his Greek island. Once there she found herself faced with trading her innocence for freedom!

Practical Dreamer by Dixie Browning

Thane Coulter shattered Tally's poised professional front whenever he came near, and yet, he was the only man who could pick up all the pieces.

Two Faces Of Love by Mary Carroll

Marcello's insistent love-making had dazzled Gina, but his enigmatic behavior was breaking her heart. Gina realized too late that she was in love with a man who didn't need her.

A Private Eden by Ashley Summers

Upset that Gabe had deceived her, Sara no longer knew what to think about the man she found so seductively attractive . . . but who continued to elude her love.

Hidden Isle by Ruth Langan

Morgan was capable, sincere, and in love with screenwriter Kent Taylor. Alone with him on his Canadian island retreat, she longed to show Kent her love—before he left the island and her life forever.

Delta River Magic by Edith St. George

Powerless to say no to Chase Barrister, her handsome, enigmatic boss, Francine accompanied his godmother on a cruise down the Mississippi. Only Francine didn't realize she'd be accompanying Chase as well!